The Suspect Speaker

James Stephens

Published by DMS Publishing, 2021

ISBN: 978-0-473-56624-1

This is a work of fiction.

Similarities to real people, places, or events are entirely coincidental.

THE SUSPECT SPEAKER

First edition. March 14, 2021.

ISBN: 978-0-473-56625-8 (Epub)
ISBN: 978-0-473-56626-5 (Kindle)
ISBN: 978-0-473-56624-1 (Softcover)

Written by James Stephens.

Acknowledgements

Melissa Brazier: *Speech Language Therapist*
Naomi Bondi: *Speech Language Therapist*
Andrea Robinson: *Registered Music Therapist*
Janet Thomson: *Eurythmy Therapist*

AphasiaNZ esp: Emma Castle and Kate Milford
(http://www.aphasia.org.nz/)
Wellington, Hutt and Kāpiti Aphasia Community

Megan Glass: *Registered Music Therapist*
Penny Warren: *Registered Music Therapist*
SoundsWell Singers
(facebook.com/SoundsWell-Singers-705452049615491/)

Penelope Todd: *editor*
(https://www.penelopetodd.co.nz/manuscripts-sought/)

And my whanau: my wife, children (six of them) and
grandchildren (another six of them!) who were
magnificently patient, supportive and kept me grounded!

The Suspect Speaker

There are fifteen short **short** stories in this volume.

All the stories are about people who have difficulty in verbal communication.
People with aphasia.

Aphasia is the loss of a previously held ability to articulate ideas or comprehend spoken or written language, resulting from damage to the brain caused by injury or disease.

These stories contain a taste, an inkling, of what it is to have aphasia: the frustrations, the anger, the acceptance and the blessings.

People with aphasia have individual communication difficulties:

> Some can't read very well, or their attention span is fatigued.
> Some have lost some vision.
> Some can't write but their vocabulary is adult.
> Some can't find the sense in syntax, or they lack context or comprehension.
> Most understand the words, but can't pronounce them.

Each story here has three versions: A, B and C.

The A version is for people who have aphasia that have difficulty in reading. The sentences are compact and descriptions are sparse.

The C versions is for people with aphasia who can read, or who like to be read to, by their supporters/carers.

The B versions are in-between – a therapeutic 'sandwich'. People who have aphasia can get the gist of the stories from the A version, and in recovery, over time, can extend their reading ability for the B or C stories.

The Suspect Speaker

1:

Shore

1A: Shore

I had walked along the beach.
It was cool. I wore a hat and a jacket.

I looked at the wave's debris.
So many varieties of seaweed.
So many seashells.
So many varieties of rubbish.

On the beach beside me was a dead shag.
A gutted fish.
Parts of a crab and a lobster.
A gruesome sight.
I was shocked.

The worst was the dead shag. Its neck was
clearly broken. Its wings torn off.

Flies buzzed around.

I sat on a rock, contemplating.

Someone was approaching.

The girl, about ten years old, was poking
with a stick.
Then, she stopped.
I knew what she had seen.

She was looking at the shag.

She cried out. She fell and grazed her knees.
I went over to her. To help.

"Are you alright? Can you get up?"
That's what I meant to say.
Actually I said, "Awwl-rit? You? Get you out
…um…up?"

The girl looked at me with fear.
I felt a hand on my jacket.
A woman spun me around.
"What did you do?" she said.

"No..no…thing nothing. She…I…went,
wanted help…"

"You're drunk! Get way from her!"
She glared at me.

I gestured, a *No! No!* signal.

"Get away! Get away from us!" the woman
said.

I backed away. I shrugged.
I knew that the woman wouldn't understand.

I turned and lurched down the beach.

I am a gutted fish.
A broken-necked shag.

1B: Shore

I was on a rock, contemplating.

I had walked along the stony beach between the waves and the bushes. It was cool.
I wore a dirty hat on my head and a grubby jacket. The wintry sun was almost warm.

I looked at the debris that had washed in the ceaseless waves. So many varieties of seaweed. Some looked like leather, others like lettuce. So many seashells, crabs and feathers. So many varieties of rubbish.

On the beach beside me was a dead shag, a gutted fish, and parts of a crab and a lobster. They were placed in an arc. It was gruesome.

I was shocked at the violence inherent in the scene. The crab was on its back. The lobster shell had been smashed. The fish had been filleted. Its lifeless head was still intact.

The eyes were eaten out. The tail was fanned out. The rest of its body was gone.
The worst was the dead shag. It's neck was clearly broken. Its wings had been torn off. Myriads of flies buzzed around.

I sat on a rock. Contemplating the ocean and the land. *The ocean: relentless, inexhaustible. The land: solid, fixed. This battle has been fought for aeons.*

I became aware that someone was approaching. The girl was wandering, tunelessly whistling. She was poking with a stick at the seaweeds, shells and pebbles. Every so often she would pause and examine a treasure.

Then, she stopped. I knew what she had seen. She was looking at the fish, the lobster, the crab. And the shag.

Shocked, she cried out and stumbled. She grazed her knees. She cried out again.

I went over to her, to help. "Are you alright? Can you get up?" That's what I meant to say. Actually I said, "Awwl-rit? You? Get you out …um…up? Hmm…?"

The girl looked at me with fear. I felt a rough hand on my jacket. A woman spun me around. "What did you **do**?" she said.

"No..no… nothing. She… I…went, want help him…her!" I indicated to the girl. "Help she."
"You're drunk! Get way from her!" She helped her daughter up. She glared at me. I gestured, a *No! No!* signal.

"Get away! Get away from us! " She backed away, dragging her daughter with her.

I backed away too. I shrugged. I knew that the woman wouldn't understand. I lurched down the beach. Away from the conflict.

I am a gutted fish. A broken-necked shag.

1C: Shore

I was on a rock, contemplating the ocean and the land.

I had walked along the stony beach between the wash of the waves and the coarse grasses and salt-stunted bushes that bordered the farmland. It was cool, and I wore a dirty red woollen hat over my hair-sparse head and a grubby jacket. I had grabbed them from the hooks beside the door of the bach. As I walked the pale, wintry sun marginally warmed me.

Clambering over the rounded rocks I noticed that several vehicles had been along the beach and impacted the stones into firm tracks. Sometimes it helped my progress, sometimes not.

I looked at the detritus that had washed in the ceaseless waves.

So many varieties of seaweed: greenish, brownish, reddish, blackish, feathered, bulbous, smooth and shiny. Some looked like leather, others like lettuce.

So many seashells: limpets, cockles, pipi, tuatua, turret shells, pāua – whole, broken, faded or fresh. And so many animal fragments: crabs, kina and lobster shells, feathers.

So many varieties of rubbish: plastic bottles and bottle tops; ties made from rubber tubes; wooden poles; nylon fishing lines tangled up into an immense Gordian Knot.

A gruesome sight halted me.
On the beach beside me was a dead shag, a gutted fish, and parts of a crab and a lobster.

They were placed in a semicircle, laid on top of a tangle of leathery seaweed. Some of the seaweed had been ripped up, roots and all, and still clinging to the rock that had anchored it.

It was a ghastly vignette. A terrible tableau. I wondered: *Surely they'd been **placed** there. Was this a demented art project?*

I was shocked at the violence inherent in the scene.

The crab was on its back, legs splayed out and inert pincers frozen. Only half of the lobster was visible. It legs were broken and its shell had been smashed. I thought the fish was a gurnard. It had been filleted. Its lifeless head was still intact but the eyes had been eaten out, I expect by a gull. Its spine was an arc of bones and bits of silvery flesh. The fluted tail was fanned out as it was swimming, unaware that the rest of its body was gone.

The worst was the dead shag.
Its neck was clearly broken and it had been dismembered. It was unclothed, naked, the feather cloak torn off. Raped by the casual nonchalance of the sea. *Indifferent ocean*, I thought.

Myriads of flying insects buzzed around. Kamikaze pilots with no-one at the control tower.

I walked up the beach. I sat on a rock, contemplating the ocean and the land.

The ocean: relentless, inexhaustible, hungry, patient ... arrogant?
The land: solid, fixed, stoic, sentinel ... exhausted?
The ocean and the land. The ages, the aeons that this battle has been fought. The birds, the fish, the animals – even the seaweed – were pawns in this ageless Armageddon.

Someone was walking along the same stretch of beach.

The girl was meandering, tunelessly whistling. About ten years old, she was meandering, poking with a found stick at the seaweeds, shells and pebbles that had washed up on the beach.

Every so often she would pause and examine a treasure: the vibrant rainbow in a pāua shell; a strand of Neptune's necklace; a feather, iridescent in the wintery sun.

Then, she stopped. I knew what she had seen: the gutted fish, the lobster and the crab. And the dead shag.

Shocked, she cried out and stumbled. She fell awkwardly onto rock, grazed her knees and cried out again.

I went over to her, to help. Catching my shoe on a rock I almost stumbled myself. I righted myself and approached her quickly.

"Are you alright? Can you get up? Is anyone here for you - your mother or father?"
That's what I meant to say. That was what I thought to say.
Actually I said, "Awwl-rit? You? Get you out ...um...up? Hmmm. Our ... your...mum ...?"

The girl looked at me in panic.

A hand landed on my jacket. Roughly.
A woman spun me around. "What did you
do? What did you **do**?" she said.

"No…no…thing…nothing. She…I…went,
want help him… her… Help just…wanted,
help!" I indicated to the girl. "Fowl…fall over.
Fell. Help she."

"You're drunk! Get away from her!" She
glared at me. She hauled her daughter up
and wrapped her arm around her shoulders.

I held out my palms, gesturing with the
universal negative signal. *No! No!*
But my words were still tongue-tied.
"I…I…not..no…I help. Help hur!"

"Get away! Get away from us! You're drunk!"
The woman backed away, dragging her
frightened daughter with her.

I backed away too. I shrugged, a helpless
gesture.
My hat, my jacket, my stumbling, my
speech…

My appearance and manner gave force to her assumptions. The woman wouldn't understand about my aphasia.

My suspect speech.

I turned away. Dejected. Tears of regret coloured my vision.

I lurched down the beach, away from this conflict.

I am a gutted fish.
A broken-necked shag.

2:

Avoidance

2A: Avoidance

Pene said, "Dubble wump?"
The couple were puzzled.

"Dubble wump?" Pene said again with a shrug of her shoulders.

The couple turned and went on their way.

Thank goodness, Pene thought. Her "made-up" language had saved the day.

Pene avoided conversation. She had aphasia. An unwelcome guest.

Confused, wrong words. Conversation was too hard.

So, she avoided talking with strangers.

"Hey?" A tall man was approaching.

"Hey! Missus?" he called.

Pene went the other way.
"Hey, wait up," he said.

Pene caught a foot and fell on the pavement.

The man was concerned.
"Hey missus! Are you okay?"
He helped her up.
He held something in his hand.

 "Um … you left your wallet behind at the café!"

She shook her head.
So embarrassing, she thought.

She looked at him.

"Wump?"

2B: Avoidance

"Dubble wump, ori dubble warhnet?" Pene said.

The couple who had stopped Pene to ask for directions looked puzzled.
"Dubble wump?" Pene said again with a shrug.

The couple glanced at one another.
They muttered something and carried on down the street.

Thank goodness, Pene thought.
People couldn't cope with other languages.
Not even made-up ones.
She went in the opposite direction, towards the town.

After Pene's stroke, aphasia had made a home in her brain. An unwelcome guest.

Mispronounced, confused or wrong words. She was tired of the effort to communicate. It was too hard.

So, she avoided conversations with strangers. When confronted, she shrugged and said "Dubble wump?"

"Hey?" A tall man was approaching her. He wore a hat, T-shirt, shorts and sandals. "Hey! Missus?" he called.

Pene ducked her head and hurried on. "Hey, wait up," he said.
Pene wove through the pedestrians. She glanced back at the man. He was following. Pene increased her pace, but the man was keeping up with her.

Pene caught her foot on a paving stone and fell to the pavement. The man caught up. Pene would have said "Dubble wump?" but the fall had confused her.

The man's face was concerned.

"Hey missus! Are you okay?"
He reached out to help Pene up.

In his other hand was something familiar.
"Um … you left your wallet behind at the café!"

She shook her head.
So embarrassing, she thought.

She looked at him.
"Wump?" she said, forlornly.

2C: Avoidance

"Shi mank dubble wump," Pene said. "Dubble wump, ori dubble warhnet?"

The couple who had stopped Pene to ask how to get to the museum looked perplexed. Their jaws dropped down like cartoon characters.

"Dubble wump?" Pene said again, fake-forlornly, with a shrug of her shoulders.

The couple mumbled a quick apology, excused themselves and carried on down the street.

Thank goodness, Pene thought. *Another tedious conversation averted. English-speaking people couldn't cope with other languages. Not even made-up ones.*

Pene went in the opposite direction, towards the town, in search of anonymity.

Exit, pursued by a bear. She smiled to herself with the aptness of the literary quote.
Actually, more grimace than a smile.

After Pene's stroke, aphasia had made itself at home in her brain. An unwelcome guest.

Aphasia.
Mispronounced, or misarticulated words.
Misordered or miscomprehended syntax.
Misappropriate contexts.
'Mis-Mis-Mis-Mis-...' reverberated in her mind.

The condition taxed her. She was tired of the effort communicating called for. It was too hard. In the end, she avoided conversations with strangers. Beggars looking for change. Hare Krishna book-sellers. Survey takers. Charity-workers seeking donations. Greenpeace-Amnesty International-World Wildlife do-gooders.

When confronted, she resorted to a "Dubble wump?" and an elegant shrug of her shoulders.

"Hey! Missus?"

As if commanded, she turned. A tall man was approaching her. He wore a shapeless, rainbow-coloured hat. His hair was a straggly mess of curls and his greying beard fell to his chest like a tangled fishing net. His t-shirt and shorts were stained and his hairy bare legs ended with worn leather sandals.

"Hey! Missus?" he called again. Pene ducked her head and kept walking.

"Hey, wait up."

Pene wove between pedestrians. Surely the persistent figure would give up in the crowd and go away? She surreptitiously glanced back. He was still following – skipping, hopping, almost running to catch up.

Pene increased her pace.
The scruffy man matched her tempo.
Actually, he was accelerating.

"Hey! Hey, Missus?" he called.

Pene caught her foot on a paving stone and sprawled onto the pavement.
Several people came to help.

"Okay!' she said, "Okay! Am roo … riii…Am all-right! " shaking off the well-wishers.

The scraggly man had caught up. Pene searched for her made-up language, but the fall had rattled her.
Even her "Dubble wump" had evaporated.

Intellectually abandoned, she resigned herself and faced the man. The sandalled, stained shorts and T-shirt man. The rainbow-coloured hatted man. The scruffy, scraggly, straggly haired and grey-bearded man.

But concern was written all over her pursuer's face. "Hey missus! Are you okay?"

He reached out a hand to help Pene as she struggled to her feet.

In the other hand was something familiar. "Um … you left your wallet behind at the café!"

She shook her head with mortification. *So embarrassing*, she thought.

She looked at him.

"Wump?" she said, forlornly.

3:

Bum

3A: Bum

Her bum's hanging out.

Ryan was walking behind two women on the main street of the city.
One was a mature woman and the other was younger. *Mother and daughter?*

The younger woman had a leather bag slung over her shoulder.

But – that was the problem.

The bag had trapped her skirt, which had ridden up against her hip.
Someone should tell her.

People passing him were apparently unaware. Most were blank-faced.
And no-one was volunteering to help.

He had to do something.

Reaching her, he said, "Excuse me!
Your bag has hitched up your dress."

Well, that was what he wanted to say.
Actually he said, "Scuse. His bag… is…up…
up…hmmmm…"

The girl looked at him with alarm.
"Sorry?" she said loudly.
The older woman said, "What is going on?"

Both looked at Ryan.
Slow down! he told himself.
"Your…bags…hitch. Up," he slowly said.

The girl looked down.
Blushing, she adjusted the bag and her
dress.

They turned and marched away along the
pavement.

Ah, well, he thought.
At least I did something.

3B: Bum

Her bum's hanging out.

Ryan was walking behind two women on the main street of the city. One was a middle-aged woman and the other was younger. *Mother and daughter?* Ryan speculated.

The woman had a red beret and a black leather jacket. She wore a tartan skirt and red leggings. She carried a clutch purse. *Very elegant.*

The other woman had loose, long hair. She wore a blue vest over a pale short dress. Her long legs were bare. She had strappy shoes. *Fashionable.*

She had a leather bag slung over one shoulder. But – that was the problem. The bag had trapped her skirt, which had ridden up against her hip.

And so: *Her bum's hanging out.*

Well, almost. *I didn't mean that, exactly,* Ryan thought, but it's what his brain had come up with. His next thought was: *Someone should tell her.*

He looked all around for someone, preferably a matronly woman. People passing him seemed unaware. Most were blank-faced. Some were grim-faced and unsmiling. And no-one was volunteering to help.

He had to do something.

Ryan hopped and skipped around other pedestrians. Reaching the young woman, he said, "Excuse me! Your bag has hitched up your dress."

Well, that was what he wanted to say. Actually he said, "Scuse. His bag… is…up… up…hmmmm…"

The girl looked at him with alarm. "Sorry?" she said loudly.

The older woman said, "What is going on?"

Both looked at Ryan accusingly.
Their expressions said, *What is this man saying? Is he drunk?*

"I...had...have...had...stroke" he explained forlornly. "Su-rri! So-rriii."
Slow down! he told himself. *Slow down!*

With a rising hand gesture, he said: "Your... bags...hitch...up."

The girl looked down. Blushing, she adjusted the bag and her dress.
The older woman gave Ryan a furious look, as if he was to blame.

They turned and marched indignantly away along the pavement.

Ah, well, Ryan thought.
At least I did something.

3C: Bum

Her bum's hanging out.

Ryan was walking behind two women on the
city's main street. On this fine, summery day,
they were striding along oblivious to the
passing shops. One woman was middle-
aged and the other was younger.
Mother and daughter? Ryan speculated.
Apparently on a mission.

The older woman wore a red beret on her
stylish brunette bob and a black leather
jacket that reeked of money. Her tartan skirt
was in muted autumn colours, with red
leggings above black ankle boots. In one
hand was a clutch purse, just right for a
mobile phone and several credit cards.
Very elegant, Ryan thought.

The younger woman's loose burnt orange
hair cascaded over her shoulders like a
sunset. She wore a blue cropped open vest
over a short and diaphanous dress, with

rainbow-coloured fish on it. Her long legs were bare, and strappy shoes raised her above the crowd.

Fashionable, Ryan thought.

A leather bag was slung over one shoulder. *Big enough to hold a laptop, two magazines, a makeup bag and a salad*, Ryan deduced.

But – that was the problem.

The bag had trapped the shimmery skirt against her hip and it had ridden up.

And so: *Her bum's hanging out.*

Well, almost. *I didn't mean that, exactly,* Ryan thought. That was indelicate, but those were the words his brain came up with.

In hindsight, with the luxury of considered thought, he could *say: 'Her rump was almost naked'* or maybe: *'Her buttocks were almost exposed to the passers-by on the street'.*

But, on the spur of the moment, Ryan's brain could only formulate: *Her bum was hanging out.* His next thought was: *Someone should tell her.*

He turn this way and that, searching for someone who could tell the girl about her clothing crisis. Preferably a matronly woman or a contemporary. The pedestrians around him were a potpourri of the city's demographic: young, old, middle-aged, male, female, with every conceivable ethnicity.

People passing him seemed unaware of the young woman's predicament. Most were blank-faced as if they were looking at a TV screen. Some were grim-faced and unsmiling, as if they had smelt something rotten. Or dead. *Maybe they have*? Ryan thought gloomily thought. *Zombified!*

And no-one was volunteering to help.

I have to do something, he thought, so he increased his pace.

As if the pair were aware of Ryan pursuing them, they increased their tempo too. Ryan hopped and skipped around other pedestrians and closed the gap. Reaching the girl's shoulder he said, "Excuse me! Your bag has hitched up your dress. You may want to adjust it."

Well, that was what he wanted to say. Actually he said, "Scuse. His bag… is…up… up…hmmmm.."

The girl looked at him with alarm. "Sorry?" she said loudly. "What?" Her elegant companion looked at him as if he was an insect. "What's going on?" she said.

Both looked at Ryan accusingly. Their co-joined expression clearly said: *What is this middle-aged man saying? Is he drunk?*

"I … had…have…had….strrrok," he explained forlornly. His indicated that his throat was blocked."Su-rri! So-rriii" Ryan said.

Slow down! he thought. *Slow down!*

"Your…bugs…hits…hit-chd…up. Up," he slowly said, with a rising hand gesture. "Bugs. Bags. Hitch-ed…Up."

The girl looked behind her at her bag and the expanse of rump exposed. Blushing, she adjusted the bag and her dress. Her presumed mother gave Ryan a furious look, as if he was the culprit. They turned and marched indignantly away as if nothing had happened, disappearing into the crowd.

Ryan was bemused. *Ah, well*, he thought. *At least I did something*.

4:

Torture

4A: Torture

Make it stop!
Make it stop!

The woman was attacking Alison.
Alison was sure her bones would be broken.

The woman had seemed pleasant enough.
She had gestured for Alison to take the sofa.

"Lay down," she commanded. "On front."

Like a lamb, Alison obeyed.

Like a tiger, the woman attacked.

At the beginning, the pressure was firm but
bearable.
Then uncomfortable.
Then painful.
Then excruciating.

I can't believe her strength, Alison mused.

Yet another torture began.
Her legs and hips were attacked.
Ah! Make it stop! Alison thought.
She shut her eyes but the pain was still there.

The misery continued.

Then – relief.
The woman had left.

Maybe the attacks would stop? she thought.
Maybe I can escape?

The woman returned.
"On back," she ordered.
Meekly Alison obeyed.

The torture began again.

Legs, torso, arms, neck, scalp…
Battering, bruising…
*Please God! Make it **stop!***

Then it was over. The woman left.

In the waiting room Alison's best friend
met her.
"That was **wonderful!**" she enthused.
"I could go **every week**! What about you?"

Alison caught her best-friend's eye.
*My **ex**-best friend*, she thought.
Alison's aphasia was severe. She grunted.

"Ah!" the ex-best friend replied.
"Next time I'll tell her to take it easier
on you."

Alison thought two things simultaneously.

Shall I reinstate my best friend?
And: *Thai massage? **Never again!***

4B: Torture

Make it stop! Please! God! Make it stop!

The woman was attacking Alison.
She worked her hands into Alison's back as
if it was play dough. Surely her bones would
be dislocated or shattered.

The woman had seemed pleasant enough.
She had smiled pleasantly and taken her to a
pleasant room. She gestured for Alison to
take the sofa. The sun was shaded by cotton
curtains. Alison glimpsed a cabinet. Above it
she glimpsed a sculpture. *A shrine?*

"Lay down," she sternly commanded.
"On front."

Like a lamb, Alison obeyed.

Like a tiger, the woman attacked.

At the beginning, the pressure was firm but bearable. Bearable became uncomfortable. Uncomfortable became painful. Painful became excruciating.

I can't believe the strength of her hands, Alison mused. The brief thought was speedily replaced by pain. Her legs, hips and buttocks were being assaulted.

Ah! Make it stop! Make it stop! Alison pleaded in her head. She shut her eyes but the pain was still there.

Shoulders. Left arm. Right arm: bearable, uncomfortable, painful, excruciating.
Surely now it will stop, thought Alison.
No, no! Neck and scalp.

Then – relief.
The woman had left.

Maybe the attacks will stop? she thought.
Maybe I can escape?

But the woman returned.
"On back," she ordered.

Meekly Alison obeyed.

The torture began again.

Legs, torso, arms, neck, scalp… Battering, bruising…
Bearable, uncomfortable, painful, excruciating…
*Please God! Make it stop! Make it **stop!***

Then it was over. The woman left.
Alison speedily gathered her things and left the dungeon.

In the waiting room Alison's best friend met her. Alison couldn't take in her friend's comments. Eventually she heard what she was saying.

"That was **wonderful!** I loved it!" she enthused. "I could go **every week!** What about you?"

Alison caught her best-friend's eye.
*My **ex**-best friend*, she said to herself.

At last her friend understood. "Oh no!
You should have told her!"

Alison's aphasia was severe. She could only
coo, hum and grunt. She shook her head
and grunted her displeasure.

"Ah!" her ex-best friend said. "I forgot!
Next time I'll tell her to take it easier on you."

Alison thought two things simultaneously.

*Maybe she could be an **ex**-ex-best friend?*
And: *Thai massage?* ***Never again!***

4C: Torture

Make it stop! Please! God! Make it stop!

The woman was attacking Alison, pummelling her back. She worked her hands into her flesh like it was play dough. Surely her bones would be dislocated or shattered.

The woman had seemed pleasant enough. She was tiny and she smiled pleasantly. She had nodded a pleasant greeting before leading Alison to a hallway. There were several doorways and she opened one to reveal a pleasant room. There was a raised sofa in the middle and she mutely gestured, pleasantly, for Alison to take her clothes off and sit down. And she, pleasantly, left the room.

As requested, Alison removed her clothes and folded them on a chair, and sat down. The bright afternoon sun was shaded by cotton curtains – a leafy bamboo pattern in olive green. In the room she glimpsed a wooden cabinet with many drawers and cupboards. Above it was a sculpture and a vase of flower. *A shrine?*

But Alison's perusal -- and her equanimity – was curtailed when the woman returned. "Lay down," she commanded, gesturing to the sofa. "On front."

Like a lamb, Alison obeyed.
Like a tiger playing with her prey, the woman attacked.

At the beginning, the pressure was firm but bearable. Then the woman worked with increasing force on every centimetre of Alison's torso. Bearable became uncomfortable, uncomfortable became painful, painful became excruciating.

I can't believe the strength of her hands, Alison mused. *And she's quite petite.* This brief academic thought was speedily replaced by her awareness of pain as yet another torture was administered.

Her legs, hips and buttocks were systemically assaulted.

Ah! Aa-aa-ah! Ooh! Make it stop! Please, God, make it stop! Alison said. In her head. She shut her eyes. The pain was a dull, red colour in her brain.

The misery continued.
Shoulders: bearable, uncomfortable, painful, excruciating.
Left Arm: bearable, uncomfortable, painful, excruciating.
Right Arm: bearable, uncomfortable, painful, excruciating.

Surely now it will stop, thought Alison.

No, no! Neck and scalp: bearable, uncomfortable, painful, excruciating.

Then – relief.

Alison became aware that the tiny woman had gone. *Maybe the attacks will stop?*

Alison didn't open her eyes, but she opened her senses. Radar-like, her awareness scanned the room. *Maybe I can escape?*

As she formulated a plan, the woman returned.

"On back," she sternly ordered.
Meekly Alison obeyed.
The torture began again.

Bearable, uncomfortable, painful, excruciating…Legs, torso, arms, neck, scalp… Battering, pressing, pummelling, bruising…Bearable, uncomfortable, painful, excruciating…

Make it stop! Please God! **Make it stop!**

Then it really was over. The woman left. Alison felt stupefied. Barely conscious, she speedily dressed, gathered her things and left the dungeon.

In the waiting room Alison's best friend was waiting for her. They left together.

Alison felt so harrowed by the shocking experience she couldn't take in her friend's chatter. Eventually she realised what she was saying.

"That was **wonderful!**" she enthused. "I **loved** it! What a **treat!** I could go **every week!** Every **day**! What about you?"

Alison caught her best-friend's eye. Mutely, she conveyed her torment gesturing to her the agony in her calves, her bruised upper arms, her mangled neck. *My* **ex**-*best friend*, resonated in her mind.

At last her friend understood. "Oh no! You should have told her! You should have said it was too hard."

Alison grunted. She looked hard at her ex-best friend, willing her to understand.

Alison's aphasia was severe. She could only coo, hum and grunt. She wanted to tell her ex-best friend that she had grunted to the masseuse, but the woman took as assent.

"Ah!" the ex-best friend replied. "I forgot!
Next time I'll tell her to take it easier on you."

Alison thought two things simultaneously.

Maybe she could be an **ex***-ex-best friend?*
And: *Thai massage?* **Never again!**

5:

Asleep

5A: Asleep

The boy didn't want to go to sleep.

He was only fourteen months old, and in a
pram. His mother – my daughter – was
determined he would, **finally,** sleep.

We were walking the trail around the local
lakes.
The boy had watched us feeding a duck.

At the playground he played on two
seesaws.

In the pram his head was nodding, but his
grip was firm.
The boy didn't want to go to sleep.

At last his concentration wavered.
He was drowsy.
But still he gripped the pram.

I sang 'La lala la-a-aa. La lala la-a-a.'

My daughter looked at me, frowning.

I wanted to explain but words fail me – now.
Since my stroke. My encounter with aphasia.

At last he entered dreamland.
Carefully, she laid her son on the blanket.

"Finally!" she muttered. She took off with the
pram. Caught unawares, I ran.

Other memories invaded my mind.
More than fifty years ago, I had to run to
keep up with my father. I was only ten.

My father, my daughter.
It was odd to think that, after fifty years, I still
had to run to catch up.

I raced after them, tripped and fell across the
path.
I woke the baby.

Well, the boy hadn't wanted to go to sleep
anyway.

5B: Asleep

The boy didn't want to go to sleep.

He was only fourteen months old, but his grip on the pram's safety bar was steadfast. His mother – my daughter – was determined that, with the pram's assistance, he would, **finally**, sleep.

We were walking the trail around the local lakes The boy had watched us feeding a duck. The duck had fussed around our feet. She quacked loudly and raucously. The boy guffawed!

At the playground he played on two seesaws. He tried each of the four seats before clambering down.

In the pram, his head was nodding, his eyes were barely open, but his grip was firm. The boy didn't want to go to sleep.

At last his concentration wavered. He was drowsy. My daughter coaxed him to relax, to snuggle down into the blanket. But he still gripped the bar as if it was a safety line. He uttered a loud cry that threatened to ruin our walk.

I sang, "La lala la-a-aa. La lala la-a-a…"

My daughter looked at me, frowning.

I wanted to explain that at least I could sing a **wordless** lullaby. I wanted to explain, but words fail me – now. Since my stroke. Since my encounter with aphasia.

At last the boy entered dreamland. Carefully, she laid her son on the blanket. Carefully, she adjusted the covers. Like a duck, I was hovering around to see if I could help.

"Finally!" she muttered.
She rapidly took off with the pram.

Caught unawares, I ran to match her speed.

Memories invaded my mind.
More than fifty years ago, I had to run to
keep up with my father. I was only ten.

My father, my daughter.
It was odd to think that, after fifty years, I still
had to run to catch up.

I raced after them, tripped and fell across the
path.

I woke the baby.

Well, the boy hadn't wanted to go to sleep
anyway.

5C: Asleep

The boy didn't want to go to sleep.

He was only fourteen months old, but his grip on the pram safety bar was steadfast. His mother – my daughter – was stoical, and determined that, with the pram's assistance, he would, **finally**, sleep.

His natural curiosity had him swinging to and fro, left and right, up and down, looking at everything. Like someone watching tennis – volleys and up-and-unders and backhanders, back and forth, back and forth.

We were walking the trail around the local lakes, dodging duck and goose poo on the path. We'd gathered loquat fruit from a neighbouring tree and the boy watched us feeding the Muscovy duck with it.

The duck fussed around our feet. The boy giggled. She quacked raucously.
He guffawed!

At the playground he had disdained the swing in favour of the seesaws. There were two seesaws. He tried each of the four seats for three oscillations before clambering down. He didn't much like the teetering tottering motion. I admired his diligence and persistence.

We convinced him to return to the pram. His head was nodding like a pigeon's, his eyes were barely open, but his grip was resolute. The boy didn't want to go to sleep. We marched purposefully on the winding path.

At last his concentration wavered. He was drowsy, his vision vacant, his face expressionless. My daughter kept coaxing him to relax his upright position and snuggle down into the comfort and warmth of the lambswool blanket. But he gripped the bar as if it was his safety line. Three, four, five times he resisted her gentle efforts.

Each time, he uttered a syncopated cry that threatened to ruin the careful rhythm of our walk.

I wanted to placate the child, so I sang, "La lala la-a-aa. La lala la-a-a…"

My daughter's evil eye censured me.

I wanted to explain…

I wanted to explain that I appreciate her care of her son.
I wanted to explain that, despite her tiredness and exhaustion, I think she's doing a tremendous job raising him.
I wanted to explain that I treasure my memories of her, at the same age as my grandson – she was quite stubborn as well.
I wanted to explain that at least I could sing a **wordless** lullaby.

I wanted to explain …. but words fail me.
Since my stroke.
Since my encounter with aphasia.
Because. Words. Fail. Me. Now.

My daughter persisted and at last the boy entered dreamland. Carefully, she laid her son on the woollen blanket. Carefully, she adjusted the covers and placed the pillow, just so. Carefully, she placed the transparent cover over the pram so the wily wind could not disturb the boy.

Like the Muscovy duck, I hovered in case I could help.

"Finally!" she muttered. She took off with the pram, prestissimo!

Caught unawares, I upped my tempo to something like a hopping, skipping, bouncing jaunt.

Other memories invaded my mind.

Fifty years ago, I had to hop, skip and bounce to keep up with my father. He was always a fast walker. I was only ten. Basically, I had to run to keep up with him!

My father, my daughter.

It was odd to think that, after fifty years, I still had to run to catch up.

I wanted to explain that amusing thought to her. Somehow.

I raced after them, reached them, tripped and fell across the pram's path.

I woke the baby.

Well, the boy hadn't wanted to go to sleep anyway.

6:

Loneliness

6A: Loneliness

Tim was lonely.

Not alone.

He had family and friends.
They talked and argued and discussed.
Tim had aphasia. He couldn't keep up.

It made him frustrated.
And lonely.

This realisation hit him at the beach.

Bryce, Tim's son, was playing in the waves
with his two children, Anna and Chris.

Tim was making a sandcastle.
He paused and looked at the ocean.
He saw a big swell three waves back.
Tim said, "What…that…this it…"

"This is a **big** one!" Bryce trumpeted.

Suddenly… the realisation.

No-one else could understand Tim's feelings. His memories, ideas or inspirations could not be shared with anyone else.

He thought: *Without verbal communication? How can I share my memories, thoughts and ideas?*

Tim suddenly felt depressed. And lonely.

Seawater drenched him.
Little Chris was the culprit.
Anna reached out her hand. "C'mon Papa!! Come swim with us!"

He looked at the children tugging on his hands.
Tim grinned. "Sure. Sure!"
Live in the moment, he thought.

"C'mon!" Tim shouted.
"Splash! Splosh! Splash! Splosh!" he said.

And they did.

6B: Loneliness

Tim was lonely.

Not alone.
He had family and friends all about him.
They talked and talked and explained and
argued and discussed.

Tim had aphasia. He couldn't keep up.
By the time he was ready to contribute...
they had moved on. It made him frustrated.
And lonely.

This realisation hit him at the beach.

Bryce, Tim's son, was playing with his two
children, Anna and Chris. They were gleefully
jumping waves.

Tim was digging a hole in the sand under the
shade of a sun umbrella. He was making a
sandcastle.

He paused and looked at the ocean.
He looked at the swells and anticipated the incoming rollers.
There was a big swell three waves back.
Tim said, "What..that…this it…"

"This is a **big** one!" Bryce trumpeted, and giggled as the children screeched.

Close by, a bird was wading in a pool left by the outgoing tide left behind.
Tim said, "What…look..look at this…the wings… the look…".

For the others, his comments didn't register.
The bird flew away.

Suddenly…the realisation.
The sloppy seaweed scalp massage!

No-one else could understand his feelings.
Not exactly. What the memories or ideas or inspirations meant to him could not be shared with anyone else.

He thought: *Some author said,* 'The past is a foreign country; they do things differently there.' *My past, my memory, my feelings are not only a foreign country, they are another planet!*

With such limited verbal communication, how could he share his memories, thoughts and ideas?

Tim suddenly felt superfluous. Depressed. And lonely.

Suddenly, seawater drenched him.
Little Chris was the culprit. He stood there, grinning, with an empty bucket.
Anna reached out her hand. "C'mon Papa! Come swim with us!"

Bryce called, "Look after the children and I will get lunch from the car."

Tim looked at him.
Bryce hesitated. "Are you okay?"

Tim looked at his grandchildren tugging at his hands. He grinned.
"Sure. Sure!"
Live in the moment, he thought.

"C'mon!" Tim shouted.
Somethings are easy to say.

"Splash! Splosh! Splash! Splosh!" he said.

And they did.

6C: Loneliness

Tim was lonely.

Not alone.
He had family and friends all about him.
But sometimes they were too much.
They talked and talked and explained and
argued and discussed and complained and
chattered and gossiped and talked and
talked.

Tim had aphasia. He couldn't keep up.
His ideas flourished, but he couldn't express
them. When he got a thought, he ran through
the wording in his head, searching and
checking the appropriate words, the syntax,
and the possible problem of pronunciation.
Then he was ready to contribute...but they
had moved on.

It made him frustrated, exasperated,
anxious, depressed. And lonely.

This realisation hit him at the beach. Like a piece of sloppy seaweed suddenly straddling his scalp.

Bryce, Tim's son, was playing with his two children in the tame surf.

Almost-four-year-old Anna was wallowing in the water and post-two-year-old Chris was clinging to his father's hand. They were gleefully jumping waves as they broke, smashed and sloshed amongst them.

Tim was digging a hole in the sand in the shade of a sun umbrella. He was piling and dribbling the wet sand into a monumental sandcastle. Sand roads, sand paths, sand canals and sand buttresses crisscrossed his construction site. A tidal pool of seawater was replenished periodically by the waves that reached the outskirts of his fortress.

Tim paused and looked at the ocean. The waves were regularly irregular. He looked at the swells and anticipated the incoming rollers.

Love is the seventh wave, he sang in his own mind, the melody drifting across years and years.

He saw a big swell three waves back. "This is a big one!" Tim said. Well…that was what he said in his mind.
Actually, he said: "What..that…this it…"

"This is a **big** one!" Bryce trumpeted, and giggled as the children screeched their terror, tempered by trust.

Tim had an inkling something was wrong, or unsteady, or unsettled. Something was… somehow…lost? He looked around at the vast sea, the endless beach, the boundless sky, searching for something…indefinable.

Close by, a bird was wading in a pool left by the outgoing tide left behind.

Look at that bird – a grey heron. It's beak is long and its legs are so slender. He's looking for fish and crabs. Mostly, they're solitary.

When heron's fly, the wings move in slow motion, he said – in his mind.

He actually said, "What...look..look at this... the wings...the look...".

His comments didn't register with Bryce, Anna and Chris. They were having fun in the surf, splashing in the waves.

The bird flew away. In slow-motion!

Tim was alone with his thoughts. He recalled one very early morning in the South Island, on a lake. It was chilly. A mist cocooned him. The trees were silhouetted by the rising sun, a light-infused smudge behind the hills.

Suddenly he saw a kōtuku, the white heron. It was like a phantom, emerging from the mist. It flew with a lazy but graceful and regal action. *A balletic, poetic gesture.* Then the bird melted into the mist again. It was only a moment – a phrase rather than a sentence.

Tim shut his eyes and opened them wide, confirming the reality of what he had witnessed. *It was wonderful*, he recalled. *Angelic. Sacred.*

His reminiscences were so palpable, so obvious. He looked at Bryce, Anna and Chris, jumping the surf and giggling. *Obvious for me, oblivious for them.*

Suddenly… the realisation.
The sloppy seaweed scalp massage!

No-one else could understand his feelings. Not exactly. What memories, ideas or inspirations meant for him, and the feelings they entailed, could not be shared with anyone else. He could indicate concrete objects with a few words. He could even gesture or draw what he was thinking about.

I can say 'bird'. I can even say 'grey heron' if they are patient enough, he thought, *but no-one knows about that sacred kōtuku. I can't say it. I can't write it. I can't draw it.*

I can't express to anyone that feeling or the meaning of that memory.

Tim concentrated on this abrupt awareness.

Some author said, 'The past is a foreign country; they do things differently there.' *My past, my memory, my feelings are not only a foreign country, they are another planet! Another dimension!*

When I says things to Anna and Chris, my words are foreign, a garbled translation.

He could hug them, smile at them, and they appreciated it. But communication? Verbal communication? How could he share his memories, thoughts, ideas and information to all of his family and friends? The years and years of knowledge and experience were …lost.

Tim suddenly felt superfluous. Depressed. And lonely.

Seawater suddenly drenched him.

Little Chris was the culprit, recklessly grinning above him with the empty bucket dangling from one hand.

Anna reached for his hand. "C'mon Papa!" She pulled him up from his sandy catacomb. "C'mon Papa – come swim with us!" Chris reached for the other hand.

Bryce called, "Look after the kids and I'll get lunch from the car."

Startled, Tim looked at him. Bryce hesitated. "Are you okay?" he said, with a question in his eye.

Tim looked at the expectant children tugging on his hands. He grinned. "Sure. Sure!"

Live in the moment. Whanau. That's all that matters.

"C'mon!" Tim shouted. Somethings are easy to say.

He scooped his grandchildren in his arms
and ran towards the waves.

"Splash! Splosh! Splash! Splosh!" he said.

And they did.

7:

Distancing

7A: Distancing

We were walking in our bubble.
Social distancing.
We can walk our streets for exercise.
Local streets.

Some people approached. They crossed the
road and passed on the other side.

My wife muttered, "'Social distancing'
should be 'physical distancing'."

I know what she means.
I always know what she means.

Our routines have been suspended.
I reflected: Weekdays, weekends, hardly any
traffic.

My wife picked up on my thoughts.
She often does that.

"It's like Christmas morning" my wife said.

I struggled to answer.
"Gud…Gud Frideh…Fri…Day."
She listened. She always listens.
"Good Friday?" She got it. "Yes…gloomier.
Good Friday. Or ANZAC Day."

We walked down the street, crossing the
road to the park.
Wooden posts were in the grass to prevent
cars coming in.

"What day is it?" my wife said.
"My undy…wear is Weddeh," I replied.

Puzzled for a moment, she then laughed.
I had seven pairs of underwear each with the
name of a weekday on their elastic band.
"Weddeh," I confirmed.

We linked hands. We walked across the park
to another road.

We saw another couple.
They crossed the road.

"Kia ora!" my wife called boldly.
Startled, they looked up.
"Hi!" they said in tandem.

We crossed the road, turning right into the street.
Whoops! I realised, *I got it wrong.*

"Sorry – I will....would...the street...."
I began again.

"The street was in-fused...what...were I...got..."

Begin again again! S l o w l y .
"Sorry...I thought...the cor...ner was...before...it was."
In my mind I said, *Damn it.*

My wife smiled.

She knows what I mean.
She always knows what I mean.

7B: Distancing

We were walking in our bubble.

Social distancing. Isolating.

"Keep the virus at bay – keep safe – keep in your bubble," my wife declared.

The mantras were reassuring.
Sort of, I thought.

We can walk our streets for exercise. Local streets. Within a few blocks of our home.

Some people approached. They crossed the road and passed on the other side.
We greeted them with a gesture. They were not keen to connect but at last they responded. No words.
It was weird.

My wife muttered, "At work we've decided that 'social distancing' should be 'physical distancing'." She is in the health sector.

I know what she means.
I always know what she means.

Our routines have been suspended.
I reflected: *Weekdays, weekends, only essential work, no school, hardly any traffic. Every day is a holiday.*

My wife picked up on my unspoken thoughts. She often does that.

"It's like Christmas morning. No traffic..." she said.

No – not a holiday, I thought. There is an atmosphere of dismay.
I struggled to answer.
"Gud...Gud Frideh...Fri...Day."

She listened. She always listens. And she got it. "Good Friday? Yes...gloomier. More like Good Friday. Or ANZAC Day."

We walked on, crossing the road to the park.
Wooden bollards squatted in the grass to
prevent cars from entering. We walked down
the meandering path.

"What day is it?" my wife asked.
"My undy…wear is Weddeh," I replied.
Puzzled for a moment, she then laughed.
I had seven pairs of underwear, each named
with a day of the week on their elastic band.
I scanned for the name.
"Weddeh," I confirmed.

We linked hands. We walked across the park
to another road.
The homes were varied, but similar.
Maybe the same developer? I thought.

We saw another couple. Heads down, eyes
averted, they crossed the road.

My wife crossed the line!
"Kia ora!" she called boldly.

Startled, they looked up.
"Hi!" they said in tandem.

We crossed the road, turning right into the street.
Whoops! I realised, *I got it wrong.*

"Sorry – I will…would…the street…"
I began again.
"The street was in-fused… what was…the street…were I…got…"

Begin again again! S l o w l y . . .

"Sorry… I thought .. the cor..ner was…before …it was."
In my mind I said: *Damn it.*
That was the best I can do.

My wife smiled.

She knows what I mean.
She always knows what I mean.

7C: Distancing

We were walking in our bubble. 'Locally'.
Social distancing. Isolating.
Two metres apart.

"Keep the virus at bay – keep safe – keep in
your bubble – stay home – be kind – save
lives," my wife declared.
"That's what Auntie Jacinda says."

The mantras were reassuring.
Sort of, I thought. *Omnipresent and ominous.*

The pandemic lockdown prescribes that we
can only walk our streets for exercise.
Local streets. Within a few blocks of our
self-isolating home.

Some people approached. They crossed the
road and passed on the other side.
We glanced and greeted them with a casual
but careful gesture. They were not keen to
connect – heads down, eyes averted – but at
last they responded.

A wave. A thumbs up. A nod/flick of the head. No words. It was weird.

My wife muttered, "Maybe they think that 'isolation' means 'total isolation'. Talking across the road is no risk." She plunged on. "At work, we've decided that the term should not be 'social distancing' but 'physical distancing'. That should be the description." She is in the health sector. "People can be social, but two metres apart. Apart from coughers. Or spitters."

I know what she means.
I always know what she means.

This lockdown has disrupted our quotidian life. Our routines have been suspended. I reflected: *Dormant. Quiescent. Hibernating. Weekdays, weekends, only essential work, no school, hardly any traffic.*

My wife picked up on my unspoken thoughts. She often does that. "It's like Christmas morning.

"Everyone is in their homes, only a few people on the street, no traffic…"

No – it's not a holiday, I thought. *There is an ambient pall over our lives.*
Over our environment and psyches.
A damper of dismay.

I struggled to answer.
"Gud….Gud Frideh… Fri…Day."

She listened. She always listens.
"Good Friday? Ah!" She got it. "Yes … yes… it is more sombre. Gloomier. More like Good Friday. Or ANZAC Day."

In the dusk, shadows were creeping like stalking cats. The sun was slinking below the horizon. A dirty, reddish hue infused the few wind-whipped clouds. We walked down the street, crossing the road to the park. Wooden bollards squatted in the grass to prevent cars from entering.
Sentinels. Gnomish guardians.

A path meandered across the unkempt grass. "I guess the lawnmower man is locked down too," my wife surmised. The leaves of the deciduous trees were muddy-green with patches of red and yellow. Autumn was approaching.

"What day is it?" my wife said.

Speedily, I cast my memory back to this morning. "My undy...wear is Weddeh," I replied.

Puzzled for a moment, she then laughed. I had seven pairs of underwear, each with the name of a weekday emblazoned on their elastic band. I placed them in the drawer ranked in order of the days.

Surreptitiously, I checked. I could see a sunny, golden fabric on the elastic band and I scanned the name, even though it was upside down. I couldn't speak "Wednesday" but I could recognise it!
"Weddeh," I confirmed.

We linked hands. We walked across the park to another road, making our circuitous route back home. My wife has no sense of direction. She would get lost in a paper bag, as they say. My sense of direction is infallible.

The urban homes are varied, but similar. The design aesthetic was identical: tile roofs, wooden boards above concrete bricks, the house parallel to the pavement, two-car garages, standard mail boxes. *Maybe the same developer? Architect? Builder? Certainly the same vintage.*

We saw another couple. Heads down, eyes averted, they crossed the road.

My wife crossed the line!
"Kia ora!" she called boldly.
Startled, they looked up. "Hi!" they said in tandem. A smile. A wave.

"Physical distancing not social distancing!" my wife muttered.
I squeezed her hand confirming my support.

We crossed the road, turning right into the
street.
Whoops! I realised. *I got it wrong. Not so
infallible!*

I took her elbow and turned her in the
opposite direction. Her look questioned me.

"Sorry. I will...would...the street..."
I began again.
"The street was in-fused...what was...the
street...were I...got..."
Begin again again! S l o w l y . . .
"Sorry... I thought ... the cor...ner was...
before ...it was."
In my mind I said: *Damn it. That was the best
I can do.*

My wife smiled, demurely.
She knows what I mean.
She always knows what I mean.

97

8:

Walkway

8A: Walkway

The walkway beckons.

I haven't been on this path before.

There is a map.
The path leads to a café in the village.
Maybe they have muffins?

The path is snaking around the shore.
Maybe I should say 'eeling'.
Eels are common. No snakes in Aotearoa.
So, the path is eeling around.

The tide is almost out.
Herons, oystercatchers and seagulls are
feeding.
The bush is soaks up the noise from the
highway.
I relax and breathe the fresh air.

A mother with a toddler in a pushchair approaches.

"Kia ora! What a beautiful morning!" I say.

Actually, what I said is, "Kee ahh ! Beauu… hmmm!"

The mother thinks I'm retarded.
The child wants to look at me.

A couple is approaches, walking a dog.
The dog growls and barks at me.

I pass a seat but I don't need of it.

Two men are jog up behind me.
They jog past.

A kingfisher sits beside a stream.
He flies away.
A beautiful bright blue and green arrow.

The sunshine is peaceful. I breathe deeply.

Then, I spy an obstacle.

The café is out of reach.

Because there is a stairway.
Twenty or more steps.

And I am in a powered wheelchair.

My legs and one arm are paralysed.
Because of my stroke.
Because of my aphasia.
Because of the thing that derailed my life.

Disappointed but resigned I turn back.
On the eeling path.

But now I long for a cup of coffee.
And a muffin.

8B: Walkway

The walkway beckons.

I haven't been on this path before. There's a car park is beside the highway. There is a map. The path leads to a café in the village. *Maybe they have muffins?*
There are three toilets. *Very convenient.*

The path is snaking around the estuary. *Maybe I should say 'eeling'. Eels are common. No snakes in Aotearoa.* They have the same motion. So, the path is eeling around between the bush and the shore.

The tide is almost out.
Herons, oystercatchers and seagulls are feeding. Two spoonbills, half a dozen swans and a dozen ducks and are dabbling.

The bush is soaking up the noise from the highway. The cabbage trees are in bloom.

The perfume is divine. I relax and breathe the refreshing atmosphere.

A mother with a toddler in a pushchair approaches.
"Kia ora! What a beautiful morning!" I say.
Actually, what I said is, "Kee ahh ! Beauu… hmmm!"

I think the mother thinks I'm retarded.
The child is stretching his neck to see me.
Apparently, I'm amazing!

A couple approach. They're walking a dog.
The dog growls and barks at me. As they pass the couple apologise.

I pass a seat but have no need of it.

Suddenly I hear footfalls and harsh breathing. Two men are jogging behind me.
They jog past.

The path crosses a small stream.
A kingfisher is beside the stream.
He flies away.

A beautiful iridescent blue and green arrow.

I continue along the eeling walkway. The sunshine is a balm. So relaxing. I breathe deeply.

Then, I spy an obstacle.
The walkway is very good. But the café is out of reach. Because there is a stairway. Twenty or more steps.
And I am in a powered wheelchair.

My legs and one arm are paralysed. My speech is paralysed too.
Because of my stroke.
Because of my aphasia.
Because of the thing that derailed my life.

Disappointed but resigned I turn back. Along the same eeling path. The sunshine, the air, the bush, birds and the view are breathtaking.

But now I long for a cup of coffee.
And a muffin.

8C: Walkway

The walkway beside the estuary beckons with the promise of comfortable solitude.

I haven't been on this path before. A car park beside the highway can handle four cars. *Maybe five, if they were small.* There is a map that promises to lead from this point to a café in the village. *Excellent. Maybe they have muffins?* There are three toilets – mens, women's and a paraplegic toilet.
Very convenient.

A path leads away from the highway, following a bushy hill. Beside the estuary.
Perfect.
The path is snaking around the estuary.
Maybe I should say "eeling". In Aotearoa eels are common here, whereas snakes are in zoos. And eels have the same sinuous, serpentine, supple-spine snake-like locomotion.

So, the path is eeling around the estuary
between the bush and the shore.

The tide is almost out.
Herons, oystercatchers and seagulls are
feeding on crabs, snails and other delicacies.
Two spoonbills, half a dozen swans and a
dozen ducks are dabbling and feeding on
the sea grass. The seagulls squark at each
other, squabbling over morsels. The rest are
concentrating on their kai moana.

The bush is soaking up the noise from the
highway, generating physical and spiritual
oxygen. Pōhutukawa, kōwhai, pūriri, karaka,
kohekohe, kawakawa. And the interlopers:
gorse and broom, ragwort and thistles.
Tī kōuka – the cabbage tree – are in bloom.
The subtle perfume is divine.

The highway clamour is fading away. I relax
and breathe the refreshing ambience.

A mother with a toddler in a pushchair
approaches.
The infant is gazing at me.

"Kia ora! What a beautiful morning!" I say.

Actually, what I said is, "Kee ahh ! Beauu… hmmm!"

I think the mother thinks I'm retarded. She stares me, puzzled and anxious. Fixedly. I nod at them both. They carry on, but the child is craning his neck to see me. Apparently, I am amazing!

A fish jumps. The ripples expand and dissipate. I look for another fish. *There! Whoops – not a fish*. A shag pops out of the water like a jack-in-the-box. He flicks his wet-feathered head back as if it was gelled, looks around, and dives again.

A couple approaches. They are walking a dog – a foxy-cross. The dog growls and barks at me. I attempt to say the things that people say to dogs and infants but the dog is not convinced. As they pass, the couple are apologetic.
I pleasantly say "Hmmm" at them.
Never mind.

I pass a seat but have no need of it.

I hear footfalls and harsh breathing. Two men are jogging up behind me. They skirt around me and, with a "Kia ora", they jog past. The echoing sounds fade.

The path crosses a small stream. A kōtare, kingfisher, is on a rock beside the stream. He flies away. *A beautiful iridescent blue and green arrow. Apparently the joggers were not threatening but I am,* I guess.

I continue up the eeling walkway. The sunshine is a balm. So relaxing. I breathe deeply. The air is so clear and revitalising. The view is magnificent.

It is good to be away from the city's bustle, noise and traffic. And the attention. A relief.

Then, I spy an obstacle. *Damn.*

The walkway is very good. Excellent.
But the café is out of reach.

Because there is a stairway. Twenty or twenty-five steps.
And I am in a powered wheelchair.

My legs and one arm are paralysed.
My speech is paralysed too.
Because of my stroke.
Because of my aphasia.
Because of the thing that derailed my life.

Damn, bugger and blast it. So close.
Ah, well...

Disappointed but resigned, I direct my wheelchair to turn around, making sure to not go in the sea! I return. On the same eeling path. As before, the sunshine, the air, the bush, birds and the view are breathtaking.

But now I have a longing for a cup of coffee.
And a muffin!

9:

Poem

9A: Poem

"Why was the monkey swimming?"

I looked over at Angela aged six.

"What…mon-key?" I asked.

When I talk, I have to talk slowly.

"The thing that Grandma told me."

We were returning from a visit to my mother.
She moved to the beach after my father
died.

She had a tidy cottage.
Outside roses and vegetables grew in the
garden.

"Working in the garden gives me some
exercise," she said.
But her back and knees are aching.

Angela and I come to visit my mother.
I do what I can to help.

I looked at Angela. "What…po-em?" I said.

"The poem that Grandma said to the picture."

I understood. *The picture of the Virgin Mary and the infant Jesus.*

"What Grand-ma…doing?"

"She said 'Blest to a monkey swimming.' Why was the monkey swimming?"

It became clear. *Not a poem, but a prayer.*
I ransacked my brain.

Hail Mary, full of grace.
The Lord is with thee.
Blessed art thou amongst women, and blessed….
Amongst women. A mon-key s-wimming.

I chuckled.

9B: Poem

"Why was the monkey swimming?"

I looked over at Angela. She was six years old. She had a puzzled look.

"What...mon-key?" I questioned her. When I talk, I have to concentrate and talk slowly. I often mix words up.

"The one in the poem. The thing that Grandma told me."

We were returning from a visit to my mother. We had travelled from our home in Wellington to Raumati Beach. The sea was restless and relentless. Rain was threatening. The horizon was invisible. Kāpiti Island was a faint shadow.

My mother moved to the beach after my father died. In the tidy cottage, her room is filled with photographs, pictures, books.

Angela's and my photographs take pride of place on her dresser. My father's and my wife's are relegated to the back.

Outside roses, camellias and gardenias ring the cottage. Across a lawn there was a vegetable garden: lettuces, beans, cabbages, tomatoes.

"Working in the garden gives me some exercise," she says.
Despite her garden "exercise", her back and knees protest. Angela and I come to visit my mother. I do what I can to help.

At my mothers place Angela is calm and steady, listening to Grandma's rambling. So, travelling back home, I was surprised about her puzzled look.

"What... po-em?" I asked.
"The poem that Grandma said to the picture."
"Which...pic-tit-ture?"
"The one in Grandma's bedroom."

I understood. *The picture of the Virgin Mary and the infant Jesus.*
"What…Grand-ma…was it…what he… she was doing?"

"She wanted to be kneeling. Then she spoke a poem. She said, 'Blest to a monkey swimming.' Why was the monkey swimming?"

It became clear. *Not a poem, but a prayer.* I ransacked my brain. The prayer emerged.
 Hail Mary, full of grace.
The Lord is with thee.
Blessed art thou amongst women, and blessed….
Amongst women. A mon-key s-wimming.

I chuckled. *But what should I say to Angela? Poem? Prayer?*

"I liked the orange roses at Grandma's house" Angela said. "They were beautiful."

Whew. Problem averted.
This time.

9C: Poem

"Why was the monkey swimming?"

I looked over to Angela in the passenger seat. There was a puzzled look on her six-year-old face. Maybe it was contagious, because I was conscious that my face now wore the same expression.

"Mon-key? What mon-key?" I questioned her.

Angela knows that when I talk, I have to concentrate on each syllable and talk slowly. And I often mix words up. Angela is very patient!

"The one in the poem. The thing that Grandma told me."

We were returning from a visit to my mother. We had travelled the sixty kilometres from our home in Wellington to Raumati Beach, a pleasant drive along the west coast despite the stormy weather.

The sea was restless and relentless. On one side of the narrow highway, waves pounded the rocks. On the other side bush-lined slopes towered. Rain was threatening. The horizon was invisible – the greys of ocean and sky were identical. Kāpiti Island was a faint shadow. *A spectre of its shadowy past,* I mused.

My mother moved to the beach after my father died, fifteen years ago. She has a tidy U-shaped cottage: living room, kitchen, laundry and bathroom in the middle with a bedroom wing each side.

Her room is filled with photographs, pictures, cushions, books, knick-knacks and memorabilia – the flotsam and consequence of her life. Facing her bed, a sturdy crucifix and a picture of the Virgin Mary are prominent.

Angela's and my photographs take pride of place on her dresser. My father's and my wife's photographs are relegated to the back. My mother doesn't like Mary, my wife.

And I'm not sure about my father.

The other bedroom is pristine. "In case someone wants to stay," she says. But no one has been in that room for fifteen years.

Both bedrooms and the living room had sliding doors that opened out onto a covered patio. "The conservatory" as my mother calls it.

Outside, there is a surprising garden, given the proximity of salt air and sandy soil.

Roses, camellias and gardenias ring the 'conservatory' and across a pocket-sized lawn there runs a vegetable garden: lettuces, beans, cabbages, tomatoes. I have encouraged her to rip out the lawn and install a raised vegetable bed but she insists that she likes it this way.

"I like my lawn-mower man. It's the charitable thing to do. And working in the garden gives me exercise."

I contend that the 'charity' is the $50 that she gives to the lawn-mower man each fortnight. And despite her garden 'exercise', her back and knees are protesting. She is stubborn.

So, once a month, Angela and I come to visit my mother. I do what I can to help: tighten screws, clean gutters, reach things on the top shelves, clean cobwebs from the ceiling, dig some garden and turn the compost.

At home, Angela is a boisterous, lively soul, bubbling with energy. But at my mother's place she is calm and steady, listening to Grandma's rambling. I am constantly amazed by my daughter's perspicacity, her prescience, her uncanny ability to appropriately adjust to any situation. Angel-a indeed!

So, travelling back home, I was surprised about her puzzled look.

"What …. po-em?" I asked.

"The poem that Grandma said to the picture."

"What…which…pic-tit-ture?"

"The one in Grandma's bedroom. The lovely lady. With a veil. With the baby. Stepping on the dragon."

My puzzlement deepened – until I twigged.

The picture of the Virgin Mary and the infant Jesus, stepping on a snake, a personification of the devil.

"What Grand-ma … was is…what he… what…she was doing?"

"She wanted to be kneeling. I helped her because her knees are stiff. Then she spoke a poem. I think she said it to my Mum."

"What?" I almost missed a corner.
Concentrate on the road. "Why did why …
you think … was… Mum?" I said, awkwardly.

"It began with 'Hey Mary', and other stuff.
And then she said 'Blest to a monkey
swimming.' Why was the monkey
swimming?"

It became clear. *Not a poem, but a prayer.*
Hail Mary, full of grace…

I ransacked my Catholic cobwebbed brain.
So many years ago… But the prayer
emerged.

Hail Mary, full of grace.
The Lord is with thee.
Blessed art thou amongst women, and
blessed….

Amongst women. A mong-st women.
Amon-g-key-s-wo-mening.
A monkey swimmimg.
I chuckled.

But what should I say to Angela? Poem? Prayer? What was the difference. A poem to God? Should we get into this now? Was it the right time for a theological discussion?

"I liked the orange roses at Grandma's house" Angela said. "They were beautiful. Next time, can we pick some for Mum?"

Whew. The charming, distracting sanguineness of youth!
Problem averted.

This time.

10:

Grove

10A: Grove

The path meandered amongst nīkau palms.

Bob said, "I never imagined there were so many."

Nīkau were in every stage of maturity.

The discarded palm leaves had dropped everywhere.

Detritus, I thought. *Like dandruff.*

It was difficult to express my thoughts to Bob. Or anyone else.
Aphasia sucks.

I should give it a go anyway.

"Deee….dee-triii……." I gestured at the mess under our feet.

"Deee-what?" Bob questioned.
"Deee-ssss-desolation?"

I thought, 'The Desolation Of Smaug'!
I had read 'The Hobbit' to our children.
Now...I can't read.

"C'mon, slowcoach!" Bob called.
"We'll have lunch at the top!"

The word I was seeking popped into my
head. *Rubbish. I should have said "rubbish".*

The gravel path ascended.
Sometimes, it was a wooden boardwalk.
The trail climbed rapidly.

Bob was already several metres ahead.
"Wow! Look at the bush!" He gestured.

I was pleased to have a breather.
Thankfully, Bob was having one too.

Bob pointed in excitement. "Hey! A fantail!"
He had spotted a dancing bird in the
branches.

It was fanning and flashing its tail.
Then it dived into the air. Another fantail
arrived.

"C'mon. The picnic table," Bob said.
"I'm famished."

The bush thinned out as we reached the top.
Bob was already setting out lunch.
I sat down gratefully and looked at the view.

The bush spread out before us.
The city, sea and island were remote.
A breeze cooled my sweat.
I breathed, deeply.

Strenuous but satisfying.

"Thank...you...Bob" I said to my husband.
"Love...ly, Love...ly."

Some things are easy to say.

10B: Grove

The path meandered amongst nīkau palms.

"This is stunning," Bob said. "I never imagined there were so many here."

"Groh…." I attempted."Gruuu…vvve"
"Huh. Yeah," Bob assented. "A nīkau grove."

Nīkau were in every stage of maturity, from grass-like shoots to slender spears to muscular columns. *Another world.* Other trees were scattered about. Their extended limbs looked awkward amongst the uniform nīkau trunks.

Underneath, discarded palm leaves were everywhere. *Detritus,* I thought. *Like dandruff.*
My brain was excited. *Or a dinosaur graveyard! The skeletal remains of creatures, weaving a pattern of decay…*

My thoughts were unrestrained…but it was hard to express them to Bob.
Or anyone else. *Aphasia sucks.*

I should give it a go anyway.
"Deee….dee-triii……." I gestured at the mess under our feet. The word "detritus" was stuck in my mind.

"Deee-what?" Bob questioned. "Deee-struction? Dee…? Deee-ssss-desolation?"

I thought: *Actually, desolation was a good word. 'The Desolation Of Smaug!'*
I had read 'The Hobbit' to our children.
Now…I can't read.

I body-languaged to Bob: *It doesn't matter.*

"C'mon, slowcoach!" he called. "We will have lunch at the top!"
He turned and launched himself at the path. I followed. The word I was seeking popped into my head. *Rubbish. I should have said "rubbish". Too late.*

The gravel path ascended. Sometimes, a wooden walkway took us over boggy ground. The boards were netted with wire mesh. The trail climbed rapidly. Rocks and roots formed the steps. Bob was already several metres ahead.

At last he paused at the top of a set of steps. "Wow! Look at the bush!" He gestured at it. I turned, pleased to have a breather. Thankfully, Bob was having one too.

"I like the stowaways," Bob said. "The grasses and flax and ferns. What are they called? Epitites?"

Epiphytes, I answered in my own mind. *Airborne aerial apartments.*

Excitedly, Bob pointed into the branches. "Hey! A pīwakawaka!"

The dancing, darting bird was fanning and flashing its tail like a flamenco dancer. It dived into the air, twisting and turning, scaring insects into betraying their presence.

Another fantail arrived. I was captivated. But….

"C'mon! The last slope. Then the picnic table," Bob said. "I'm famished."

The bush thinned out as we reached the top of the ridge. Bob was already setting out lunch. I sat down gratefully. My legs ached with the a satisfying sense of achievement.

The bush spread out before us. In the background the city and traffic were remote. The sea was just a faint hue and the island was floating. A few clouds floated in the sky. The sun caressed my face. A breeze cooled the sweat on my brow. I breathed, deeply.

Strenuous but satisfying.
Effortful but peaceful.
"Thank…you…Bob" I said to my husband. "Love…ly, Love…ly."

Some things are easy to say.

10C: Grove

The path meandered, skirting the trunks of nīkau palms.

"This is stunning," Bob said. "From the road, I never imagined so many nīkau palms were in this park."

"Groh....grohhvee," I attempted. I caught Bob's eye.
"Gruuu...vvve"

"Aha!" Bob assented. "That's right. A nīkau grove. Perfect."

Nīkau were in every stage of maturity, from grass-like shoots to slender spears to muscular columns. The fronds umbrella'd us from the summer sun, prisms that shed a dappled, speckled, greenish half-light. *Another world.* Other trees were scattered about, like interlopers: miro, rimu, rewarewa, karaka, tarata...

Their extended limbs and random branches looked awkward amidst the uniform, striped ranks of nīkau trunks with their lush, symmetrically fringed fronds.

Below there was an untidy mess with palm leaves discarded everywhere, like the aftermath of a party. I thought: *The detritus of too much biomass. Like dandruff. No... more like nail clippings. Urgh.*

My brain was excited by my speculation...

Or a dinosaur graveyard! The skeletal remains of prehistoric creatures. The enormous bone-coloured skulls, the backbones of corrugated spines, the desiccated fronds like rigid ribs, weaving a pattern of decay...

My thoughts were exuberant, unrestrained, rampant...but it was hard to express them to Bob. Or anyone else. *Aphasia sucks.*

I should give it a go anyway. "Deee....dee-triii...hmmm...dee-trii-tsss...." I ventured.

I gestured at the mess under our feet. I waved at the piles of discarded fronds and their enormous bowls. The word "detritus" was stuck in my mind. *Surely there was a better word? An ordinary word?*

"Deee-what?" Bob asked. "Deee-struction? Deee-bris? Deee-tribulation? Dee...? Dee...? Deee-scards?"
Bob, bless him, was trying. "Deee-ssss-desolation?"

Actually, desolation was a good word. 'The Desolation Of Smaug!' Reminiscences flooded my mind. That was a film about Tolkien's 'The Hobbit'. I had read 'The Hobbit' to our children.
Now...I can't read. *Ah. Never mind.*

I body-languaged to Bob: *No...It doesn't matter,* eloquently shrugging my shoulders.

I looked at the detritus. Again. That word, stuck in my head.

If a nīkau frond falls in the grove as detritus, I mused, and no-one is here to hear it, does it makes a sound? A Zen question. I have no answer. *Maybe that is the point.*

"C'mon, slowcoach!" Bob called. "We will have some vittles at the picnic table at the top!" He turned, launching himself at the path.

I followed. At the same time, the word I was seeking popped into my head. *Rubbish. I should have said "rubbish".* Too late. Bob was already forging ahead.

The gravel path ascended between nīkau trunks and other native trees. Sometimes, a wooden walkway took us over boggy ground. The boards were netted with wire mesh stapled down to the timber. The stepped walkway followed the same pattern as the path, zigzagging amongst the palms and trees.

We left the saturated ground and the trail climbed rapidly. Rocks and roots now formed the steps. Bob was several metres ahead. *And several metres above me too!* I thought, puffing with the exertion.

At last he paused at the top of a set of steps. "Wow! Look at the bush! It is fabulous." He gestured grandly.

I turned, pleased to have a breather. Only a few nīkau were growing at this altitude. For the next twenty metres, the path became a shelf, set into the slope. Then steps again!

Thankfully, Bob was having a breather too.

"Look at these trees.
I like the stowaways." Bob indicated the branches above. "The grasses and flax. Orchids and ferns. What are they called? Epitites?"

Epiphytes, I answered in my mind as I gazed up. My gasping breath meant I couldn't answer anyway. *Airborne aerial apartments.*

I sat on a handy root and craned my neck to see how far we had come up. *Wow, a long way up!* I looked over my shoulder. *And a long way to go too!*

Bob continued to examine the bush. He pointed excitedly. "Hey! A pīwakawaka pīwakawaka-ing!" I'm always amused when Bob makes up words.

He had spotted the dancing, darting bird in the branches. It was fanning and flashing its tail like a flamenco dancer, pirouetting and posing on a branch, flicking this way and that. It dived into the air, twisting and turning in steep climbs and sudden drops, dive bombing like a child playing fighter pilot, scaring insects into betraying their presence.

Another fantail arrived. Then another, chirping and squeaking like a classroom of children playing plastic recorders. I was captivated. But….

"C'mon! The last slope. Then the picnic table," Bob said. "I'm famished."

The steps were oddly placed, following the contours of the rocks and roots.

A giant's pace apart. Surely a long-legged DOC ranger had created these steps! I thought ill of him!

The bush thinned out as we reached the top of the ridge. To one side there was a rude picnic table. A-frame legs supporting two slabs of wood as seats and three slabs for the table. Bob was already setting out lunch, unpacking the hummus, crackers, apples and our thermos of coffee.

I sat down gratefully. My legs ached with a satisfying sense of achievement.

I looked at the view. *Magnificent.* An eiderdown of bush spread out before us. The nīkau disappeared under the taller trees. *A hidden skeleton.* The city was remote, the traffic noise muted. The sea was a faint purplish hue in the background.

The island was floating majestically like an immense waka. A few cotton-wool clouds floated in the azure sky.

I looked up and closed my eyes as the sun caressed my face. A nuzzling breeze cooled the sweat on my brow, prickling my temples. A soothing massage.

I breathed, deeply.

Strenuous but satisfying.
Arduous but serene.
Effortful but peaceful.

"Thank…you…Bob" I said to my husband. "Love…ly, Love…ly."

Some things are easy to say.

11:

Fog

11A: Fog

Shaun awoke from his doze.

A cockroach was on his open book.

His brain seemed to be coming out of a fog.
Disgusted, Shaun brushed the insect into the
garden.

What happened? he thought.
Shaun looked around.

He was sitting outside.

Shrubs were dotted nearby.
Further away, flaxes and grasses were
carefully placed.

He looked further.
Grassy sand dunes, a golden beach, a bay.

He turned.
Behind him was a building.

An impressive structure. Whose abode?

Again, fog clouded his thoughts.

Abode? House!! he thought.
What? Why? Am? I? Here?

A woman came out of the house.
 She rapidly crossed the lawn.

"What happened Shaun?" she asked.
She is concerned, he thought.

The fog cleared.
Ah, Rose, my wife.

He said, "Ruu - Russ -Ruse."
He sighed and began again, but s l o w l y .

"Ro-se. I …o…kay."

She sat beside him on the other seat.

"Good. That's good," she said.
"What a view!"

11B: Fog

Shaun awoke from his doze.

There was a cockroach on his open book. It's feet trailed spilled red wine across the pages.

His brain seemed to be emerging from a fog.

Scrawled? he thought. *That's the right word. Scrawled!*

Disgusted, Shaun brushed the insect into the garden. He focussed on the upset wineglass. *What a waste. But what happened?*

Quickly Shaun looked around. He was sitting outside in a courtyard, on a chair, at a table. Shrubs in terracotta pots were allocated around. Beyond them flaxes and tussock grasses had been carefully placed.
Orderly. Just so.

He looked further. Grassy sand dunes, a golden beach, a bay, and a tree-lined rocky cove. Railway sleepers made a stairway connecting the courtyard to the shore.

He turned. Behind him was a building. Several sun sails shaded the deck. Windows and sliding doors gave access to the courtyard. *An impressive structure.* Shaun appreciated the angles.

Again, fog clouded his thoughts. *Whose abode? Why am I saying 'abode'? Not an abode…House! Abode = House!*

In his head he saw the equal sign. The fog lifted. *Aha! I **used** to be a maths teacher.*

But what…why? Am? I? Here? he thought, with all the question marks.

A woman came out of the house. She rapidly crossed the lawn.
"What happened Shaun? Are you okay?"
She looked puzzled.

No. Not puzzled. Concerned.
He shook off his foggy thoughts.

Rose. My wife. Rose organised this holiday for us.

He said, "Ruu - Russ -Ruse."

He sighed and began again, but s l o w l y .

"Ro-se. I…o…kay."
Shaun shrugged in a helpless gesture.

She sat beside him on the other seat.

"Good, That's good," she said, relieved.
"What a view! Do you want more wine?"

11C: Fog

Awoken from his doze, Shaun became aware that a cockroach was scaling across his open book.

The cockroach's feet trailed spilled red wine across the page.

His brain seemed to be emerging from a fog.

Scaled? he thought. No – that was not the right word. *Doodled? Nah.* The insect's path was purposeful. It was more calculated and determined. *Scrawled? Ah! That's the right word. Scrawled!* The cockroach's feet embroidered a rapid, incomprehensible calligraphy that embellished the printed words.

Disgusted, Shaun brushed the cockroach into the garden. He focussed on the horizontal wineglass, weeping wine across the table, trickling the precious merlot to the ground, dribbling it amongst the pebbles.

What a waste was immediately replaced by *What happened?*
Tendrils of fog still wove through his mind, displacing his thoughts.

He concentrated. *Receded – no. Not the right word. Suspended? Recoiled? Recoiled! Huh?* Odd, but it seemed right.
Recoiled. Appropriate. Apparently.
He commanded his 'recoiled' brain to unravel itself, to see what had happened. Before the fog.

Quickly Shaun looked around. He was sitting outside, in a courtyard, on a wicker chair, at a wrought-iron table. Decorative pebbles formed a sea, lapping at concrete tiles.
Islands, he thought.
Stepping stones. Regular.

Trimmed shrubs in terracotta pots were allocated around. Railway sleepers defined the edges. Beyond them, tidy flaxes, tussock grasses and well-groomed bushes had been carefully placed.

Orderly, he appreciated. *Just so.*

He looked further. The vista was magnificent. Sunlight enlivened the view. He saw: grassy sand dunes; a golden beach; an arc of a bay; an aquamarine sea with a moving embroidery of foaming waves; a distant tree-lined rocky cove. Railway sleepers made a welcoming stairway that connected the courtyard to the shore.

He turned. Behind him was a building. Vaulted zinc rooflines intersected with the planes and angles of walls, glass, and concrete brick chimneys. Windows and sliding doors gave access onto the extensive deck that bordered the patio.

Wow! More glass than timber. An impressive house. It was clearly an architect-designed structure.

Shaun appreciated its complexity. *The subtle system of the house's topography.*

Several sun sails shaded the deck.
The curve is catenary or parabolic?
The words were inserted in his mind with an
ease that surprised and delighted him.

Not my abode, he thought. *Whose abode?*
Why was he saying 'abode'? *Good word, but
a bit unusual.* Again, whispers of fog veiled
his thoughts. He shook his head to clear it.

*An H- word? H-? Ha-? Ho-? Hotel? Hose?
Hoose? No, no … House! Abode = House!*

In his head he saw the equal sign.
The fog lifted.
*Ah, I **used** to be a maths teacher.*
The angles, the topography, the curves.

But…what? What? Why? Am? I? Here?
inveigled itself into his brain with all the
question marks attached.

A flash of memory.
Book-a-Batch. Batch…no, bach – Bach!
Music flooded his thoughts.
Concerto for Two Violins. So exquisite…

Shaun's thoughts were freewheeling!

Concentrate...

A woman came out of the house. Red haired, fifty-ish, floral cotton-print dress, jandals. She rapidly crossed the lawn. "What happened Shaun? Are you okay?" she asked, with a puzzled frown.

No. Not puzzled, he thought. *Concerned.*

He shook off his foggy befuddlement. *Book-a-Bach. Rose organised this holiday for us. Rose, my lovely wife. Thank you. Recuperation. The sun was so soporific, I just dozed off and upset my wine glass. The view is stunning and this house, the bach, is marvellous. I appreciate the architecture of this place. It reminds me of my maths teaching. The angles, the planes and intersecting lines, the topography. I free-associated the word 'bach' to 'Bach' and I could clearly hear, in my minds ear, the Concerto for Two Violins.*
But then I realised .....

A momentary thought.

A 'momentary thought' in that it was a thought that took a moment.

He wanted to speak, to express these thoughts, but… ?

"Ruu - Russ - Ruse.…"
Aphasia rules, K-O! Concentrate…

He sighed and began again, but s l o w l y .
"Ro-se. I…o…kay." Pause. "Rell… real-ly… okay." Shaun shrugged in a helpless gesture. He pursed his lips to give an air kiss to Rose.

Her concern evaporated and she embraced her husband. She sat beside him on the other seat.

"Good, That's good," she said.
"What a view! Do you want more wine?"

12:

Lost

12A: Lost

He was lost.

Tom had left the bush track.

He had looked at the ancient trees.
Their trunks were a home for insects and spiders.
Their joined roots were exposed.

A tūī sang.
Bell-like tones descended to burping like a sound of a drunkard.
Trickster, Tom thought.
Another tūī answered in the distance.

He looked around. The track was nowhere to be seen. He was lost.

A kererū startled him when it flew up. Its wings beat the air like drums.
He became aware of an echo.

He followed the sound.

He scrambled up a bank.
Suddenly the sound was all about him.

A waterfall was plummeting twenty or thirty
metres to a gully.
The water gushed from a hidden channel
above.
Then, the stream met the rocks.

Boom-dikuh-uh-doom-dikuh-dikuh-doom-
BOOM.

Tom gloried in the sound.
The water spray acted as a prism.
Several tūī careeried about.
Kererū soared gracefully.
A gecko sunned itself on the rock only
metres away.

Suddenly – a call.
"C'mon!" Tom's wife shouted.
"Lunch is ready! If you're late the kids will
clean it up!"

He called back.

"Okay...back...it...is...was...this way...
hmm...hmmm."

His speech faltered.

With aphasia, he could only manage one or
two words.

"Time!" he called.

Tom made his way back, twenty metres to
the beginning of the official bush track.

Their car was parked there.
His wife had set out lunch on the picnic
table.

At least I was lost for a while, he thought

Lost, in the beauty of nature.

12B: Lost

He was lost.

Tom had left the bush track and made his own way down the ridge.

Overhead trees screened the blue sky with a net work of branches, twigs and leaves.

He had looked at the ancient trees, bearded with dripping moss. Their trunks were reinforced by angled wings, home for insects and spiders. The entwined roots were exposed. It seemed that the trees were rising as if they wanted to leave the ground entirely.

A tūī announced its presence. Bell-like tones descended to burping like the sound of a drunkard. *Trickster*, Tom thought.

Another tūī answered in the distance. Tom imagined they were looking down on the plodding human. *A chorus of condescension.*

He congratulated himself on that apt description. Maybe he should write it down, but he didn't have a pen or paper. After his stroke, Tom's short-term memory was suspect.
That is the way it is, he contemplated.

He looked around. The track was nowhere to be seen. He was lost.

A kererū startled him as it flew up. Its panicky wings beat the air like sudden drums. He became aware of an echo, a beat unevenly spaced.

Boom-dikuh-uh-doom-dikuh-dikuh-doom-BOOM.

Then it was repeated. Again. Again.

He followed the sound.

Skirting shrubs and sudden trenches, he scrambled up a bank.
Suddenly the sound was all about him.

A waterfall was plummeting twenty or thirty metres to a gully. The water gushed from a hidden channel above. When the stream met the rocks the collision gave rise to the repeated rhythm:
Boom-dikuh-uh-doom-dikuh-dikuh-doom-BOOM.

Tom gloried in the sound.
Almost like a mantra.

Lost, he sat and mused.
The natural sound is deafening, but is better than the noise of the 'normal' world.

The water spray acted as a prism. Rays from the bright sun rainbowed across the gully. The leaves, usually every shade of green and brown were now in yellows, reds, blues, purples.

The waterfall flowed and flowed with a dikuh-doom-BOOM.

Several kamikaze tūī careered about.
A kererū soared gracefully like a prayer.
A gecko sunned itself on the rock only metres away.

He mused: *Time doesn't exist in this space. Time is only measured by the sun, the stars...*

Suddenly – a call.

"C'mon!" Tom's wife shouted.
"Lunch is ready! If you are late the kids will clean it up!"

After the natural sounds it was demanding. Imperious.

He called back. "Okay... back...it... is....was...this way...hmm...hmmm..."

His speech faltered. He was always a man with few words but, with aphasia, he could only manage one or two.

"Time!" he called.

Tom made his way back, twenty metres to the beginning of the official bush track. Their car was parked there.

His children were playing a game of soccer on the lawn and his wife had set out lunch on the picnic table.

At least I was lost for a while, he thought

Lost, in the beauty of nature.

12C: Lost

He was lost.

Tom had left the bush track and made his own way down the ridge. Overhead, trees screened the azure sky with a lattice work of branches, a tracery of fine twigs and stippled leaves.

He had meandered, looking at the ancient trees. Bearded with dripping moss, their multi-armed limbs were frozen.
Tom thought: *Like a gesture of Thai dancers.*
Their trunks were reinforced by buttresses, supports and angled wings.
Secret places and shadowy spaces.
Home for insects and spiders.

The intertwined roots were exposed. The trees seemed to be ascending, rising from the mossy and ferny beds as if they wanted to leave the ground entirely.

Verdant clouds tentatively tethered to the earth, Tom reflected, smug at his poetic description.

A tūī announced its presence.
Exquisite bell-like tones descended followed by mechanical clicks and guttural burps like a drunkard snorting and hiccouging.
Trickster. Another tūī answered in the distance with the same phrase.
Their conversation flew to and fro.

Tom imagined they were looking down on the plodding human, pitying his flightless state and ant-like activity.
Antiphonal, professing their proclamations and pronouncements, Tom thought.
A chorus of condescension.

He congratulated himself on that apt description, arising in a moment of clarity.
He should write it down...but he didn't have a pen or paper. And he knew that his brain wouldn't remember the phrase.
It would evaporate.

After his stroke, Tom's short-term memory was suspect. *That is the way it is. Commendable acquiescence,* he thought philosophically. *Or resignation.*

He looked around.
The track was nowhere to be seen.
He was lost.

A kererū flew up and startled him. Its panicky wings beat the air like sudden drums, a prolonged roll on tympani. He became aware of a faint answering percussion. The beat was unevenly spaced. It was a syncopated but regular rhythm.

Boom-dikuh-uh-doom-dikuh-dikuh-doom-BOOM.
Boom-dikuh-uh-doom-dikuh-dikuh-doom-BOOM.
Boom-dikuh-uh-doom-dikuh-dikuh-doom-BOOM.

A minimalist rhythmic cell. Like an Indian tala. Another description he should note down before it evaporated… *Ah, well…*

He followed the sound, crescendoing with each step. Skirting shrubs and sudden trenches in the undergrowth, he scrambled up a hillock. Suddenly, it was all about him. *Surround sound. Augmented reality.*

A waterfall was plummeting twenty or thirty metres to a gully. The water gushed from a channel above, discernible in the lush undergrowth. Tom sat down, stunned by the display.

The spurting water was almost enclosed at the top of the drop, forming discrete 'bags'. As they dropped, the 'bags' lengthened and grew amorphous, collaborating with other fluid 'bags', mingling and melding in the downward flow. Then, they met the rocks.

The collision gave rise to the syncopated rhythm:
Boom-dikuh-uh-doom-dikuh-dikuh-doom-BOOM.
Boom-dikuh-uh-doom-dikuh-dikuh-doom-BOOM.

Boom-dikuh-uh-doom-dikuh-dikuh-doom-BOOM.

Tom gloried in the sound.
Almost like a mantra.
Lost, he sat and mused.
The natural sound is almost deafening, but is preferable to the chatter and noise of the 'normal' world.

He surveyed the gully. The water spray acted as a prism. Sun rays rainbowed across the chasm, multi-hue-ing the trees, bushes and grasses. Usually in every shade of green and brown, now they wore yellows, reds, blues, indigos, purples.

He meditated. *Elemental. Air and water coalesce, merge, collude in the ethereal mist surrounding this place. An actual authentic alchemy – with alliteration too!*
Without paper and pen, another evaporated phrase.

The waterfall continued to flow and flow.

Several tūī careered with kamikaze abandon through the bush. A kererū soared as gracefully as a prayer, angelic wings opening to the sky and bowing to the earth in veneration. Because Tom had been so still, he saw a gecko sunning itself on the rock only metres away.

Time doesn't exist in this space. Or actually, time is expanded in this space. Minutes, moments don't matter here. Time is only the measured by the sun, the stars and moon, the seasonal fluctuations. Time is only ….

Suddenly – a call.
The gecko scampered into the undergrowth.

"C'mon!" Tom's wife trumpeted. "Lunch is ready! Guacamole and crackers! If you're too late the kids will clean it up!"

After the natural sounds the call was demanding, insistent.
Almost imperious. Tom thought.

Then he was ashamed.

Ungrateful. Unappreciative. Ungracious.
He called back. "Okay…back…is…it…is…
was…this way…hmm…hmmm…"

His speech faltered.
Always a man with few words but, with
aphasia, he could only manage hesitant one
or two. And mostly it took several minutes to
get the words straight anyway.

"Time!" he called and then he thought: *Ironic!*

The trees, birdsong, river, the waterfall….
Time: measured by the sun, the stars and
moon.
Time: for questions with no need of answers.

Time*: for lunch….*

Tom made his way back, twenty metres to
the beginning of the official bush track and
the picnic spot where their car was parked.

His children were playing a game of soccer
on the lawn, and his wife had set out lunch
for them on the picnic table.

He was always grateful – for his wife, his children – but sometimes their conversations were exhausting.

At least I was lost for a while, he thought

Lost, in the beauty of nature.

13:

Reminiscences

13A: Reminiscences

He waited for her on the beach.

She came down the sand to join him.
She light-bathed in the sunrise.
He photographed her, like long ago.

They had been at this beach forty-five years
ago. When they were fifteen.

They celebrated the moment.

They went down the beach. The sunrise
behind them.
Memories, he thought.

He said aloud: "Today, it have, has, … is…
bin the first …"
He said to himself: *Aphasia! Ahhhgghh!*

She was patient.

He began again, slowly.
"Today…is the fifth…anni-ni-vers-sary of my…stroke…"

He looked at her.
She was looking at the sand.

"Thank…you" he said. "I appreciate…your caring. Your…patience."
A pause.
"What…would I do…without you?"

He looked at her. Her hand reached his.
The unspoken things between them were understood.
Forty-five years ago on this beach.

Memories…

The tide was halfway out.
The beach was swept clean.
She said, "Clean as a slate."

They turned and retraced their steps.

Both looked for shiny shells.
Looked at the sand dunes.
Looked at the waves.
Memories…

She said, "Where's our car?"

He gestured.
Tree branches were sticking out of the sand.
A path led to their car.

"Before, I saw…them…we go…on
th'beach," he said, awkwardly.

She didn't mind.

"What would I do without you?" she said.

13B: Reminiscences

He waited for her on the beach.

She came down the sand to join him.
The sun was emerging from the ocean like a molten sphere. She light-bathed in the sunrise.

He photographed her, like long ago.
They were at this beach forty-five years ago. They were fifteen. Then, she was a golden teenager. Now, her **inner** presence was golden.

They walked along the beach with the sunrise behind them.
They celebrated the moment and the shared memories.

He said aloud, "Today, it have, has,... is... bin the first...the anniversable...the anniv..."

He paused. He said to himself: *Speech!*
Aphasia! Ahhhgghh!

He began again.
"Today…is the fifth…anni-ni-vers-sary" he
spoke slowly, "of my…stroke…Jan…ry."
He looked at her as they strode in unison
along the beach.

She was looking at the sand.
Maybe she was looking at the past.

"Thandou" he said.
"Thank…you. Apprec-cian…"
A pause. "I appreciate … you. Your caring.
Your patience.
Would I what… I could…would…"
Again, a pause.
"What … would I do … without you?"

He looked at her as they walked. Her hand
reached for his. The unspoken things
between them were understood.
They swung along like teenagers.
Memories…

The tide was half-way out and the beach was swept clean.

She said, "Clean as a slate. Do you think that many people know about 'cleaning the slate'? The slate that youngsters wrote on with chalk. You remember we used to have a board that we wrote on. Do you think anyone has seen them lately?"

He responded in kind.
"Dalling phone…num-ber of … phone?"
She understood.

They turned and retraced their steps.
Both looked for shiny shells.
Both looked at the sand dunes and the bushes and pōhutukawa.
Both looked at the waves.

Forty-five years of shared memories.

With a note of panic, she said, "Where's our car?"

He gestured.

Three tree branches were sticking out of the sand.

A path led to their car.

"Before, I saw...them...we go...on th'beach," he said, awkwardly.

She didn't mind.

"What would I do without you?" she said.

13C: Reminiscences

He waited for her on the beach.

She came down the sand to join him.
The sun was emerging from the ocean like a molten orb, dripping golden droplets in its wake. She was facing the sun, eyes closed. She light-bathed in the sunrise.
"Ahhhh!" she said.
Surreptitiously, he photographed her.

Morning light. At the same time on the same beach, he photographed forty-five years ago when they were fifteen. Then, the sunrise gilded her sunripe, brown bikini-clad body. Now, her physical body celebrated the passage of time. Her **inner** presence was ripe and golden.
Transformed. Metamorphosed.

She, surreptitiously, was considering him with half-closed eyes.

He savoured the moment and the shared memories that belonged only to them.

They walked along the curiously summer-empty beach, the sunrise behind them. Their shadows were as substantial as memories.

He said, "Today, it have, has, … is… bin the first … the anniversable … the anniv…"
He paused. *Speech! In my mind's ear I know what I want to say, but the talking gets in the way. Aphasia! Ahhhgghh!*

She was patient. He began again.

"Today… is the 5th … anni - ver - sary," he spoke s l o w l y .
"Of my … stroke….. Jan…ry twrent-wun… Twen-ty…one." Pause.
He rechecked his vocabulary.
"First. Twenty-first. Jan-uar -ry."

He looked at her as they strode in unison along the beach. She was looking at the sand. Maybe for shiny shells, or sea-flung pebbles lit up by the sunrise. Maybe she was looking at the past and their long journey back to recovery. *Almost-recovery*.

'Thanddou" he said.
"Thank…You. Appreciat…" A pause.
"I appreciate … you. Your care. Your caring. Your patience.
Would I do what… I could…would…"
Again a pause. Checking the syntax.
"What … would I do … without you?"

She didn't look at him, but her hand reached for his. They swung along like teenagers. He looked at her. Considered her.
As if looking at a montage. A forty-five year old montage of all the times that he had looked at her. Memories…

The tide was half-way out and the foreshore was swept clean of yesterday's detritus.

She spoke. "Clean as a slate."

Non sequitur, he thought, casually surprised at the way his brain registered things that he could not voice. He didn't mind that she was not responding to his declaration. She understood him. The things unspoken between them were understood. Implicit.

"Do you think many people know what a slate is, and how it could be cleaned?"
At last she looked at him. The dance in her eyes was at once acknowledgement and acceptance of what he'd said.
An empathetic promise.

He recognised it. *Don't Panic And Carry On.*
She carried on....

"You know the slate that youngsters wrote on with chalk. 'Clean the slate'. Who knows about that now?

"You remember we used to have a board that we wrote on with our fingers or pencil. It had a plastic cover. When we took the plastic cover off, all our markings would be gone. A 'Magic Tablet'. Do you think anyone has seen them lately?"

He responded in kind.

"Stuck re…re-cord. Who knows…now…that now? Or dial…dial-ling phone noom…number of…phone?"

She understood.

They turned and retraced their steps.
The sun was fully up, and the gold had turned to silver.

Both looked for shiny shells, or sea-flung pebbles.
Both looked at the sand dunes, the sea-salted bushes, sea-salted pōhutukawa and the sea-salted grasses.
Both looked at the relentless waves washing the slate-clean sand.
Both said inconsequential words to each other. Sweet nothings. The meaningfulness was in their proximity, their closeness, not in the words.
Forty-five years of shared memories.

With a note of panic, she said, "Where is our car? Which way to the car park from here?"

He gestured.

About fifty metres ahead, three branches
were stuck in the sand like statuary columns.
Beside them, in the dunes, a path led to their
car, a tunnel through the undergrowth.

"Before, I saw…it…them…we go…on
th'beach…now," he said, awkwardly.
She didn't mind.

"What would I do without you?" she said.

14:

Bubbles

14A: Bubbles

It was the bubbles.

We were flying about 25,000 km from the dwarf planet.
Our antenna was struck by space debris.

I was an geoengineer.
Long story short, I pushed my bookie.
He struck his head on a rock.
Rather than face prison I stowed away on a rocket ship.

The *Black Roger*. A pirate ship.
The captain was Jo Sparrow.

Sparrow decided that my engineering background was useful.
I thought a 'pirate life' would be adventurous.

After six months on the *Roger,* I was over it.

The ship was a smelly, grubby, dark
dungeon.
The food and the crew were equally
distasteful.

When the antenna got wrecked, Sparrow
looked at me.
Her eyes said: *If you don't do this, I will
space you.*

In the locker I checked the suit, the helmet
and the oxygen.
And I went outside.

I repaired the antenna.
Some metal rubbish cut my air hose.
Without oxygen my muscles seized.
I was losing consciousness.....

I came to in the 'sick bay'.

Our doctor said, "Move your arms!"
 "Hu….uhh…ohh…hmmm," I said.
"Your legs!" he commanded.
"Ohh….sshu…sshh…hmmm," I said.

Lack of oxygen.
Bubbles in my bloodstream.
Bubbles.
Stroke.
And aphasia.

"What's wrong with him?" Sparrow said.
"Fix him!"
"Muhh…nooo…shuu…shuuu..hmmm," I
said.

"You can't do your job," Jo Sparrow said.
"Waste of air. Waste of space!"
So, she spaced me.

Sparrow launched me with an escape pod.

I had a secret: the escape pod had a freezing
circuit.
I could sleep until someone woke me up…

…

…

…

The pod top opens.

I'm coming out of a fog.
My thoughts are clearing.
I focus my senses.
I look at the sky above.
Purple clouds and two suns.

I look out on a strange planet.
The trees are coloured blue, yellow, orange.
Grasses cover the ground between the
trunks.
The rocks are faceted, crystalline.
The sea is lime-green and viscous.

Strange trees, strange grasses, strange
rocks, strange ocean.

A pink pyramid stands among the trees.
It is three metres high, with a two-metre
base.

I gasp. The pyramid is rolling toward me.

In my mind I say: *What are you?*
In my mind I have an answer: *What are **you**?*

I am stunned.

The voice in my mind is saying: *We would do you no harm.*

Somehow, I **know** that the 'voice' belongs to the pyramid.

I think: *What are you? Where are we?*
How can you speak to me?

The pyramid tells me: *I can see you have had many experiences you can share with us.*

I am thinking: *Talking without speaking!*

I'm in!

14B: Bubbles

It was the bubbles.

We were flying about 25,000 km from the dwarf planet when our antenna was struck by space debris. I was the obvious choice. With my background and all.

I was an geoengineer.
Long story short, my career was boring.
For excitement I gambled on the races.
My bookie roughed me up a bit, I pushed back. He struck his head on a rock.
Rather than face a prison sentence on an asteroid I stowed away on a rocket ship.

Unfortunately, it was the *Black Roger*, a pirate ship. The *Roger* had only a skeleton crew. The captain was the rough and tough Jo Sparrow. Sparrow decided that my engineering background was useful.

I thought a 'pirate life' would be adventurous. After six months on the *Roger*, I was over it.

The ship was a smelly, grubby, dark dungeon. *Black Roger*'s equipment was always breaking down. The food and the crew were equally distasteful.

So, when the antenna was wrecked, Sparrow looked at me.
Her eyes said: *If you don't do this, I will space you.*

In the locker I checked the suit, the helmet and the oxygen. And I went outside.
I found the damage and repaired the antenna. More luck than skill.

I was returning when a bit of metal rubbish flew off the *Roger* and severed my air hose.
The tether was tangled.
Desperately I reeled myself in, but without oxygen my muscles were seizing. I was losing consciousness.....

I came to in the 'sick bay'.
Our 'doctor' was a farmer. He was more used to pulling animal teeth than tending a human.

"Move your arms!" he commanded.
"Hu….uhh…ohh…hmmm…" I said in a daze.
"Your legs!" he commanded.
"Ohh….sshu…sshh…hmmm…" I was puzzled.

Brain hypoxia. Lack of oxygen. Too much nitogen and carbon monoxide. Bubbles in my bloodstream.
Bubbles.
It was all about the bubbles.
Stroke. Paralysis. Tetraplegia.
And aphasia.

"What's wrong with him?" Sparrow snorted.
"Fix him!"
"Muhh…nooo…shuu…shuuu..hmmm," I said mournfully.

That went on for six days.

"You can't do your job," Kapitan Jo Sparrow
announced.
"Waste of air. Waste of space!"

So, she spaced me.

Sparrow launched me with an escape pod.

She didn't have to do that. Maybe she had a
morsel of human dignity, but I don't think so.
The pod was cluttering up her cargo hold.

They launched me with no fuss or bother.
No speeches, no eulogies, no emotions.
I didn't expect them.

I saw the *Black Roger* spinning around me at
an ever-increasing distance.
A bright and cold star.

I had a secret. I knew that the escape pod
had a cryogenic circuit. I could sleep until
someone woke me.

I reached, painfully, desperately, for the freezing switch. At last, the button lit up. The gas filled the pod. Now, I was just going to…

….

….

….

I am coming out of a fog.

Escape pod?

The fog is thinning and my struggling senses and sluggish thoughts are clearing.

Above me is an orange sky. Purple clouds race by. *There are two suns! One golden, the other red.* Their colour illuminates the clouds.

I look out on a strange planet. The trees are spiky, in blue, indigo, yellow, orange. Grasses cover the ground between trees. Blue-green with white flowers.

The rocks are faceted, crystalline. They tower above the trees. The sea is lime-green and viscous. *No waves.*

Strange trees, strange grasses, strange rocks, strange sea.

I spy something out of place.
A pink pyramid shape placed among the trees. Three metres high, with a two-metre base. It has outcroppings and a circular 'halo'. The pyramid has deep etchings.

I gasp. The pyramid is rolling toward me. *Levitating.*

I panic and the thought comes: *What are you?*

The pyramid is halting.

In my mind I have the answer: *What are **you**?*

I am stunned.
Somehow, I **know** that the 'voice' belongs to the pyramid.

The voice in mind is saying: *We would do you no harm.*

I am thinking: *What are you? Where are we? How can you speak to me?*

The pyramid is telling me: *I can see you have so many experiences to share with us.*

I am thinking: *Talking without speaking! Excellent!*

I'm in!

14C: Bubbles

It was the bubbles.
It was all about the bubbles.

We were flying about 25,000 klicks from the dwarf planet Zefrod when our communication antenna was struck by space debris. Usually, the robo would repair the damage, but it was frizzed and on the bench, so I was the obvious choice.
With my background and all.

I was an geoengineer on the twin planet Phelok 1. Long story short, my career was tedious. For excitement I played – and gambled – on the flox races. My bookie roughed me up a bit, I pushed back, he struck his head on a rock, and rather than spend a stretch in solitary on the prison asteroid, I stowed away on the next ship leaving the planet.

Unfortunately, it was the *Black Roger,* a pirate ship, salvaging junk and plundering defenceless freighters. The *Roger* had only a skeleton crew – an ironic term, given their business. We were nominally commanded by Kapitan Jo Sparrow, a rough and tough autocrat. I'm sure the pseudonym was also ironic, being the name of a pirate 600 years ago. In the 21st Century.

Sparrow decided that my engineering background was useful, so she didn't space me. I didn't disabuse her. Actually, my engineering expertise was related to rocks and minerals and the relevant machinery.

I thought a 'pirate life' would be adventurous. How fanciful. Romantic. After six months on the *Roger,* I was over it.

The ship was a smelly, grubby, dark dungeon. *Black Roger*'s equipment was antiquated. And always breaking down. The food and the crew were equally distasteful. Kapitan Sparrow was self-serving, arrogant and brutal.

So, when the antenna was wrecked, and something or someone with an engineering bent had to fix it, Sparrow looked at me. Her eyes said, *If you don't do this, I will space you. In a heartbeat.*
I blinked.

In the locker I checked the suit, the helmet and the oxygen. I tested the thrusters and my tools. I made sure I was tethered for the space walk. And I went outside.

I found the damage and repaired the antenna. I have to say it was more luck than skill.

I was returning when a bit of metal rubbish flew off the *Roger* and severed my air hose. It was quite lucky: a handspan higher it would have smashed my helmet; a handspan to the left, it would have shredded my suit.

I held my breath and engaged the winch on my tether, but it was tangled and looped around some of the ship's superstructure.

Desperately I reeled myself in but without oxygen my muscles were seizing.
Panic stricken, I gazed frantically at the porthole. It seemed to be receding, beyond reach. I was losing consciousness…

I came too in the 'sick bay' – a couch in the dining room. Our 'doctor' was a flox farmer more used to pulling tusks out of mature floxes than tending humans. He slapped my face, shook me, and peered into my mouth, nostrils and my eyes.
In that order!

"Move your arms!" he commanded.
 "Hu….uhh…ohh…hmmm…" I said, dazedly.
"Your legs!" he commanded.
"Ohh….sshu…sshh…hmmm…" I said, puzzled.
He pulled on my ears, viciously.
"Yeooww…Ahhhh!!! I…I….Huh!…Huh!….." I cried, painfully.
"That usually works," he mumbled, "On floxes, at least."

Brain hypoxia. Lack of oxygen. Too much nitogen and carbon monoxide.
Bubbles inn my bloodstream.

Bubbles.
It was all about the bubbles.
Stroke. Paralysis. Tetraplegia. And aphasia.

"What's wrong with him?" Sparrow demanded.

I looked at her. My brain said: *I'm fine - but I can't talk. My words are scrambled and confused and I can't figure out how to work my tongue and teeth....*
I actually said, "Huh! ... Huh!... umm... Shuuu... Shuuu!"

"Hmm!" she snorted. "Fix him!"
"Muhh...nooo...shuu...shuuu..hmmm," I said, mournfully.

That went on for six days.
My arms didn't move. My legs didn't move.
My speech didn't move.

"You can't do your job," Kapitan Jo Sparrow announced. "A burden. Waste of food. Waste of air. Waste of space!"

So, she spaced me.

Actually, I was grateful. The ship, the crew, the life were abysmal. Sparrow launched me with an escape pod. She didn't have to do that. Maybe she had a morsel of human dignity – but I don't think so. The pod was cluttering up her cargo hold.

They launched me with no fuss or bother. No speeches, no eulogies, no emotions. I didn't expect them. The skeleton crew was – well – skeletons.

They ran the pod out on a metal rail and launched me into space. Sparrow called it 'walking the plank'. From my research, I know that pirates used that procedure a lifetime ago on Terra. The rest of the crew had no idea about that.

I wanted to say that I appreciated Sparrow's analogical sentiment, but: "Sent… wallnnng…ummm… walllkknnng… pllaann … huh, huh, huh, hmmm" were my last words. I am sure they didn't understand. I grinned.

The *Black Roger* was spinning around me at an ever increasing distance. A bright and cold star. I know that the spin was mine, and the increasing distance was mine, but with no gravity, no perspective, no relative motion parallaxes, my mind was deluded.
I welcomed that.

And I had a secret. Although my engineering training focussed on rocks and minerals and geological landforms, I knew about spacecrafts. I knew about escape pods. I knew that they had a cryogenic circuit. I could sleep until someone – or something – woke me.

Maybe, something or someone else could help me. Care for me. Cure me?

I reached painfully, desperately, for the cryogenic switch. At last, the button lit up. The gas filled the pod, the temperature dropped. *Snow White minus the seven dwarfs,* I thought, a memory from a long-ago childhood. Now, I was just going to...

...

...

...

I'm coming out of a...fog.
My consciousness is rising like a bubble.
I think: *Bubbles!....Just like bubbles, bursting in the sky. Bursting. Busting. Escape?*
My escape?
Think. Think.
My escape? Escape plan? Escape path? Escape ... pod?

Yes! My escape pod! I remember the escape pod. From the ship. From the Black Roger. Sparrow spaced me!!!

The fog is lifting...evaporating...and my senses and thoughts are clearing. I hear an alarm. *Descrescendoing. Is that a word? This alarming noise is ... is... the escape pod proximity alarm.* It fades with each iteration.

Then another noise. Subtle. With a whirring surround-sound, the pod top opens.
I look at the sky above.

An orange sky. Purple clouds are racing by, forming and reforming into fanciful creatures. They part for a moment and there are two suns! *One golden, the other red.* They colour the clouds with a luminescent rainbow.

Another noise. The servo in my seat is raising me to a sitting position. The air is warm. The scent is invigorating - edgy and arresting. I look around me.
Trees? Rocks? Sea?

The trees are spiky with...*leaves?*
In blue, indigo, yellow, orange.

The trunks are black with transparent, muscular veins running from ground to branches.

Grasses between the trees are variegated blue-green with white flowers. They are like drooping and dripping umbrellas.

The rocks are faceted, crystalline and somehow…more coherent. They tower in majestic columns above the trees.
They catch the glow from the suns and reflect it in a radiant gilded-crimson display. *Magnificent!*

The sea…lake…ocean? The water is lime-green and evidently viscous. *No waves, but swirls of oily currents disturb the surface.*

The colours here are dramatic, vivid. Outrageous! In ultra-rainbow hues I have never seen such potent vibrancy.
I am astonished and bewildered.

A strange planet. Strange trees, strange grasses, strange rocks, strange ocean.

I spy something out of place.
A pink pyramid placed among the trees.
A solid mass. But not like the rocks?

A strange thing amongst so many other strange objects.

It is three metres high, with a two-metre base. There are crimson feathery outcroppings about a third of the way up. *Moss? Epiphytes? Fur?*

Another third up is a circular 'halo'. *Metal? Organic?*

The pyramid is covered with deep etching marks. *Natural? Or manufactured? Decorations? Or...writing?*

I gasp. The pyramid is rolling towards me. *Over the ground. No – not rolling. Floating. Levitating!*

The etchings are mobile, fluid. *No...they are solid. Solid but fluid.* They are unfolding from the pyramid.

They look like … limbs.
With multi-fingered 'hands'.

Confused, panicking, I think: *What are you?*

The pyramid is halting.
The 'hands' are gently waving to and fro.

*What are **you**?* echoes in my mind.

I am stunned. Maybe I am crazy, but the voice in my mind is not my own!
Lucky I can't move my limbs because I would be jumping out of the pod and…

Why would you do that? the voice in mind is saying. *We would do you no harm.*

I think: *Somehow, I **know** the 'voice' belongs to the pyramid.*

Yes.

*What? Sorry? You can **read** my thoughts?*
*I'm not used to this. You're a **life** form?*

What are you? Where are we? How can you speak to me?

Ah! I see. We will take it slow. But ... know you are safe now. I am a life form. Hchkk! Hchhk! Hchhk!

The tip of the pyramid inclines toward me. *He/she/it is nodding?...or chuckling?*

He/she/it continues: *I can see you have so many experiences that you can share with us.*

We are the Alkywanna, and this planet is Meduaual ...

I'm thinking: *Talking without speaking! Excellent!*

I'm in!

15:

Panegyric

15A: Panegyric

"I thought that Neil would not talk again.

"He was paralysed. He had the clot-busting injection. It freed his limbs but his speech was gone. Neil had aphasia.

"He was a 'communication person'. His speech therapists gave him back to me. After six months he said, "The light of the moon". It was magic!

"People with aphasia are much better when they are fresh. Sometimes I had to translate his speech. Often he would say, "Takning are overright" Translation: Talking is overrated.

"I understood him better than most. But I could get it wrong.
He was looking at the newspaper. I heard him say, "Ostriches fly". I came over to see. He was saying, "Oxygen Supply!"

"He was a joke teller. He had one joke.
"What's brown and sounds like a bell?…..
Dung!!!"

"He re-invented himself. He became a
photographer.
We started biking and hiking. We saw much
more of the country.
We visited the kids and the grandchildren.

"So…thank you all so much for attending
Neil's funeral.
A lot of you have spoken to me about what
Neil meant to you.
We can talk more.

"Or not.
As Neil said, "Takning are overright'"

15B: Panegyric

"I thought Neil wouldn't talk again.

"He was paralysed. His whole right side. We were close to the hospital and he had the clot-busting injection. It freed his limbs but his speech was … absent. Neil had aphasia.

"Neil was a 'communication person'.
A businessman. A public speaker.
An organiser. A choir member.

"His speech therapists gave him back to me and our children. Though, it took a long time before he could make a sentence.
After six months he said, "The light of the moon". It was magic!

"The kids were so supportive of him too, caring and patient.

"Sometimes I had to translate his speech to other people. When our daughter married, Neil wanted to speak. He did well, but one of the groom's guests thought he was foreign.

"People with aphasia are much better when they're fresh. Morning speech is much better than evening speech. Often he'd say to me, 'Takning are overright.'
Translation: Talking is overrated.

"I understood him better than most. But, even I could get it wrong. One time he was looking at the newspaper and wanted to tell me about the article. I swear he said, "Ostriches fly." I came over to the newspaper to see what it was about. It was about oxygen and therapies. He was saying, "Oxygen Supply! Oxygen Supply!"

"He was a joke teller, but now found the timing of the punchline difficult. He had one joke that he told to everyone.
"What's brown and sounds like a bell?...
Dung!!!"

"I encouraged to look at re-inventing himself. And he did. He became a photographer. You can see his amazing photographs around the room. We started biking and hiking. We saw much more of the country. We visited the kids and the grandchildren.
"We were blessed.

"So…thank you all so much for attending Neil's funeral. I'm sure he will be looking down –or up – and be grateful for your care and thoughts.

"A lot of you have spoken to me about what Neil meant to you. Please stay on for supper. We can talk more.

"Or not.
As Neil said, "Takning are overright!"

15C: Panegyric

"Well…after the stroke, I thought that Neil wouldn't talk again.

"He was paralysed, down his whole right side, but we were close to the hospital when it happened, and he had the clot-busting injection. It freed his limbs but his speech was …well, absent. Neil had aphasia and dyslexia: a communication disorder.

"It was quite cruel. As you know, Neil was a 'communication person'. As well as a father and husband, he was a business mentor, public speaker, organiser, choir member, a joke-teller,..

"His occupational, speech and music therapists gave him back to me and our children. His singing was much better than his talking. Maybe you've heard that on his

answering phone message? It took a long time before he could make a sentence.
The first phrase he spoke clearly, after six months of therapies, was "The light of the moon". It was magic!

"The kids were so supportive of him too – caring and patient when he wanted to say things that should have taken two minutes but now took him ten.

"Sometimes I had to translate his speech to other people – his 'accent' could be a little off! When our daughter married, Neil wanted to speak to guests at the reception.
He did well, for a short time, but one of the groom's guests said to me later, "What country is Neil from?" They thought he was foreign.

"People with aphasia are much better when they're fresh. Morning speech is so much better than the evening struggle.
Unfortunately, it was the same case with me.
After a day's work, I struggled to understand

him when his night-time speech was deteriorating.

He knew that too. Often he'd say to me, '"Takning are overright."
Translation: Talking is overrated.

"Because I was always there, I understood him better than most. But, even I could get the wrong end of the stick.

"One time he was looking at the newspaper and wanted to tell me about an article. I swear he said, "Ostriches fly." I asked him and he gave the same phrase every time with all various inflections and emphases. But all I heard was, "Ostriches fly!!!"

"He was getting grumpy with me so at last I came over to have a look. The news article was about hyperbaric therapies and stroke. He was saying, "Oxygen Supply! Oxygen Supply!"

"He was a joke teller, but now the timing of the punchline eluded him. He had a stock of

one joke that he told to everyone, multiple times! I think you know it:
"What's brown and sounds like a bell?.....
Dung!!!"

"It was a delight to hear his voice again. But it was hard too. Neil wanted to be back at the same level of speech he enjoyed before his stroke. He really wanted to be back there and it was hard to watch him trying.

"I wanted to support him, but wanted to be realistic too. I told him, "I can't cope with depression! If you are depressed I'll take you to the 'Sorry' bus, and you can get on it!" Thankfully, he knows I was kidding. Sort of!

"I encouraged him to look at re-inventing himself, like Madonna, and David Bowie!

"And he did. You can see his amazing photographs around the room, the landscapes, birds and trees he captured so artistically.

"We started biking and hiking. We saw much more of the country, visiting the kids and the grandchildren. Actually, we were blessed by his aphasia!

"So…thank you all so much for attending Neil's funeral. I'm sure he will be looking down – or up – and be grateful for your care and thoughts.

"A lot of you have spoken to me about what Neil meant to you. Thank you. It means a lot to me and the children.

"Please stay on for a cup of tea or coffee and some nibbles and to reminisce.
We can talk more.

"Or not.
As Neil said: Takning are overright'"

Glossary: [alphabetical word list]

for New Zealand/Aotearoa names and terms and (maybe) unfamiliar words.

Word	Meaning	Chapter
Adult	…because their adult vocabulary is intact there is no need to 'dumb down' the words. People with aphasia aren't retarded (unless they have additional other conditions).	**Intro**
Alkywanna	Fanciful terms: an alien planet.	**14: Bubbles**
amorphous	Without a clearly defined shape or form.	**12: Lost**
antiphonal	Sung or played by two groups in turn.	**12: Lost**
ANZAC Day	ANZAC (Australian and New Zealand Army Corps) Day is a national day of remembrance in Australia and New Zealand that broadly commemorates all Australians and New Zealanders who served and died in all wars, conflicts, and peacekeeping operations.	**7: Distancing**
Aotearoa	The Māori name for New Zealand.	**General**

Word	Meaning	Chapter
Aphasia	Aphasia is the loss of a previously held ability to articulate ideas or comprehend spoken or written language, resulting from damage to the brain caused by injury or disease.	**General**
Auntie Jacinda	A nickname for Jacinda Adern, New Zealand's 40th Prime Minister from 2017 who led the country through the Covid-19 pandemic 2020/2021.	**7: Distancing**
Bubble	A term for a close family (whanau) group, popularised by the Covid-19 Pandemic in 2020/2021	**7: Distancing**
catenary or parabolic	Two curves that are similar but not identical. While a parabolic arch may resemble a catenary arch, a parabola is a quadratic function while a catenary is the hyperbolic cosine, $\cosh(x)$, a sum of two exponential functions.	**11: Fog**
cryogenic	Cryogenics is the production and behaviour of materials at very low temperatures.	**14: Bubbles**
detritus	The organic debris formed from the decay of organisms; disintegrated or eroded matter.	**10: Grove**

Word	Meaning	Chapter
eurhythmy	Eurythmy is an expressive movement art originated by Rudolf Steiner. Primarily a performance art, it is also used in education and as part of therapeutic anthroposophic medicine.	Intro
Exit, pursued by a bear.	'*Exit, Pursued By A Bear*' is a bizarre Shakespearean stage direction, leading up to the off-stage death of Antigonus in *The Winter's Tale*.	2: Avoidance
flox	Fanciful alien terms. A flox is an animal like a cross between a giant horse and a rhinoceros, with tusks. It runs very quickly and in Pheloh 1 they are used for sport racing (and betting on the outcome).	14: Bubbles
frizzed	Destroyed	14: Bubbles
Gordian Knot	The Gordian Knot is associated with Alexander the Great. It is often used as a metaphor for an impossible problem.	1: Shore
hyperbaric therapies	Hyperbaric oxygen therapy (HBOT) involves breathing almost pure oxygen in a special room or small chamber.	15: Panegyric

Word	Meaning	Chapter
Indian tala	A rhythm cycle with a specific number of beats that recur in the same pattern throughout a musical performance.	12: Lost
kai moana	Seafood (Māori)	8: Walkway
karaka	New Zealand / Aotearoa native tree.	8: Walkway
karaka	New Zealand / Aotearoa native tree.	10: Grove
kawakawa	New Zealand / Aotearoa native tree.	8: Walkway
kererū	New Zealand / Aotearoa native bird, a wood pigeon.	12: Lost
Kia ora	In New Zealand / Aotearoa (Māori) it is a warm and welcoming greeting.	7: Distancing
Kia ora	In New Zealand / Aotearoa (Māori) it is a warm and welcoming greeting.	8: Walkway
kina	*Evechinus chloroticus* is a sea urchin endemic to New Zealand / Aotearoa.	1: Shore
klicks	Kilometres	14: Bubbles
Kohekohe	New Zealand / Aotearoa native trees.	8: Walkway
kōtare	A kingfisher, a New Zealand / Aotearoa native bird.	8: Walkway

Word	Meaning	Chapter
kōtuku	New Zealand / Aotearoa native bird : a white heron.	6: Loneliness
kōwhai	New Zealand / Aotearoa native tree - it has cascades of brilliant yellow flowers in spring.	8: Walkway
Love is the seventh wave	*Love Is the Seventh Wave* is the second single and second track from Sting's 1985 solo debut album The Dream of the Blue Turtles.	6: Loneliness
mantra	A repeated word or phrase, especially in advocacy or for motivation.	7: Distancing
mantra	A repeated word or phrase, especially in advocacy or for motivation.	12: Lost
Māori	The indigenous people of New Zealand.	General
Meduaual	Fanciful terms: an alien planet.	14: Bubbles
miro	New Zealand / Aotearoa native tree.	10: Grove
Muscovy duck	Muscovy ducks are large, goose-like ducks with highly variable plumage. The bill is either pink-and-blackish and the base is surrounded by bright red caruncles.	5: Asleep

Word	Meaning	Chapter
Neptune's necklace	*Hormosira banksii* is a species of seaweed native to Australia and New Zealand.	**1: Shore**
nīkau	New Zealand / Aotearoa native palm, *Rhopalostylis sapida*, is the most southerly growing palm tree in the world.	**10: Grove**
Non sequitur	non sequitur' refers to a conclusion that isn't aligned with previous statements.	**13: Reminiscences**
Panegyric	A lofty oration (or eulogy) in praise of a person.	**15: Panegyric**
pāua	New Zealand / Aotearoa native shellfish. The pāua shell is the most colourful abalone shell in the world. Its iridescent nacre features deep blue and green hues with flashes of pink and purple.	**1: Shore**
perspicacity	The ability to understand things quickly and make accurate judgments.	**9: Poem**
Pheloh 1	Fanciful terms: an alien planet.	**14: Bubbles**
pipi	New Zealand / Aotearoa native shellfish: *paphies australis*	**1: Shore**

Word	Meaning	Chapter
pīwakawaka	(Māori) New Zealand / Aotearoa native bird - a small fan tail (English name: fantail!)	10: Grove
pōhutukawa	New Zealand / Aotearoa native tree - some call it the NZ Christmas tree because it has crimson flowers just before Christmas.	8: Walkway
pōhutukawa	New Zealand / Aotearoa native tree - some call it the NZ Christmas tree because it has crimson flowers just before Christmas.	13: Reminiscences
prescience	The ability to know or correctly suggest what will happen in the future.	9: Poem
pūriri	New Zealand / Aotearoa native tree.	8: Walkway
quotidian	Every-day	7: Distancing
rewarewa	New Zealand / Aotearoa native tree.	10: Grove
rimu	New Zealand / Aotearoa native tree.	10: Grove
robo	Robot	14: Bubbles
sanguineness	A personality trait of cheerful optimism because their attention delights in quick changes and varied ideas.	9: Poem

Word	Meaning	Chapter
Seesaws	A plank or pole with a fulcrum in the middle and a seat on either side. Some people name them a 'teeter-totter'.	5: Asleep
servo	Servo systems achieve an extremely accurate position, velocity, or torque control.	14: Bubbles
South Island	New Zealand / Aotearoa consists of two main islands. In English they are named the North Islands and the South Island. (In Māori they are more imaginatively named Te Ika a Maui, meaning the fish of Maui, for the North Island, and Te Wai Pounamu, the waters of greenstone, for the South Island.)	6: Loneli-ness
snakes	In New Zealand / Aotearoa there are no (wild) snakes. But LOTS of eels (tunā).	8: Walkway
tarata	New Zealand / Aotearoa native tree.	10: Grove
The Desolation Of Smaug	A 2013 film directed by Peter Jackson based on J.R.R. Tolkien's *The Hobbit*. Smaug was a dragon.	10: Grove

Word	Meaning	Chapter
The past is a foreign country; they do things differently there.'	The first line of *The Go-Between*, a 1953 novel by L. P. Hartley.	6: Loneliness
Tī kōuka	Cabbage tree (*Cordyline australis*) is a native tree of New Zealand / Aotearoa.	8: Walkway
topography	Topography is the study of the forms and features of surfaces.	11: Fog
tuatua	New Zealand / Aotearoa native shellfish: *paphies subtriagulata*	1: Shore
tūī	New Zealand / Aotearoa native bird. It has two voice-boxes and makes an amazing range of sounds.	12: Lost
waka	Māori watercraft, usually canoes ranging in size from small, unornamented canoes (waka tīwai) used for fishing and river travel to large, decorated war canoes (waka taua) up to 40 metres (130 ft) long.	10: Grove
Whanau	Family (Māori)	6: Loneliness
Zefrod	Fanciful terms: an alien planet.	14: Bubbles

Glossary: [by chapter]

for New Zealand/Aotearoa names and terms and (maybe) unfamiliar words.

Chapter	Word	Meaning
General	Māori	The indigenous people of New Zealand.
General	Aotearoa	The Māori name for New Zealand.
General	Aphasia	Aphasia is the loss of a previously held ability to articulate ideas or comprehend spoken or written language, resulting from damage to the brain caused by injury or disease.
Intro	adult	…because their adult vocabulary is intact there is no need to 'dumb down' the words. People with aphasia aren't retarded (unless they have additional other conditions).
Intro	eurhythmy	Eurythmy is an expressive movement art originated by Rudolf Steiner. Primarily a performance art, it is also used in education and as part of therapeutic anthroposophic medicine.

Chapter	Word	Meaning
1: Shore	Gordian Knot	The Gordian Knot is associated with Alexander the Great. It is often used as a metaphor for an impossible problem.
1: Shore	pipi	New Zealand / Aotearoa native shellfish: *paphies australis*
1: Shore	tuatua	New Zealand / Aotearoa native shellfish: *paphies subtriagulata*
1: Shore	pāua	New Zealand / Aotearoa native shellfish. The pāua shell is the most colourful abalone shell in the world. Its iridescent nacre features deep blue and green hues with flashes of pink and purple.
1: Shore	kina	*Evechinus chloroticus* is a sea urchin endemic to New Zealand / Aotearoa.
1: Shore	Neptune's necklace	*Hormosira banksii* is a species of seaweed native to Australia and New Zealand.
2: Avoidance	*Exit, pursued by a bear.*	'*Exit, Pursued By A Bear*' is a Shakespearean stage direction, leading up to the off-stage death of Antigonus in *The Winter's Tale*.
5: Asleep	Muscovy duck	Muscovy ducks are large, goose-like ducks with highly variable plumage. The bill is either pink-and-blackish and the base is surrounded by bright red caruncles.

Chapter	Word	Meaning
5: Asleep	Seesaws	A plank or pole with a fulcrum in the middle and a seat on either side. Some people name them a 'teeter-totter'.
6: Loneliness	*Love is the seventh wave*	*Love Is the Seventh Wave* is the second single and second track from Sting's 1985 solo debut album The Dream of the Blue Turtles.
6: Loneliness	South Island	New Zealand / Aotearoa consists of two main islands. In English they are named the North Islands and the South Island. (In Māori they are more imaginatively named Te Ika a Maui, meaning the fish of Maui, for the North Island, and Te Wai Pounamu, the waters of greenstone, for the South Island.)
6: Loneliness	kōtuku	New Zealand / Aotearoa native bird : a white heron.
6: Loneliness	*The past is a foreign country; they do things differently there.'*	The first line of *The Go-Between*, a 1953 novel by L. P. Hartley.
6: Loneliness	Whanau	Family (Māori)
7: Distancing	Bubble	A term for a close family (whanau) group, popularised by the Covid-19 Pandemic in 2020/2021

Chapter	Word	Meaning
7: Dis-tancing	Auntie Jacinda	A nickname for Jacinda Adern, New Zealand's 40th Prime Minister from 2017 who led the country through the Covid-19 pandemic 2020/2021.
7: Dis-tancing	mantra	A repeated word or phrase, especially in advocacy or for motivation.
7: Dis-tancing	quotidian	Every-day
7: Dis-tancing	ANZAC Day	ANZAC (Australian and New Zealand Army Corps) Day is a national day of remembrance in Australia and New Zealand that broadly commemorates all Australians and New Zealanders who served and died in all wars, conflicts, and peacekeeping operations.
7: Dis-tancing	Kia ora	In New Zealand / Aotearoa (Māori) it is a warm and welcoming greeting.
8: Walk-way	snakes	In New Zealand / Aotearoa there are no (wild) snakes. But LOTS of eels (tunā).
8: Walk-way	kai moana	Seafood (Māori)
8: Walk-way	pōhutukawa	New Zealand / Aotearoa native tree - some call it the NZ Christmas tree because it has crimson flowers just before Christmas.

Chapter	Word	Meaning
8: Walkway	kōwhai	New Zealand / Aotearoa native tree - it has cascades of brilliant yellow flowers in spring.
8: Walkway	pūriri	New Zealand / Aotearoa native tree.
8: Walkway	karaka	New Zealand / Aotearoa native tree.
8: Walkway	kohekohe	New Zealand / Aotearoa native tree.
8: Walkway	kawakawa	New Zealand / Aotearoa native tree.
8: Walkway	Tī kōuka	Cabbage tree (*cordyline australis*) is a native tree of New Zealand / Aotearoa.
8: Walkway	Kia ora	In New Zealand / Aotearoa (Māori) it is a warm and welcoming greeting.
8: Walkway	kōtare	A kingfisher, a New Zealand / Aotearoa native bird.
9: Poem	perspicacity	The ability to understand things quickly and make accurate judgments.
9: Poem	prescience	The ability to know or correctly suggest what will happen in the future.
9: Poem	sanguineness	A personality trait of cheerful optimism because their attention delights in quick changes and varied ideas.

Chapter	Word	Meaning
10: Grove	nīkau	New Zealand / Aotearoa native palm, *Rhopalostylis sapida*, is the most southerly growing palm tree in the world.
10: Grove	miro	New Zealand / Aotearoa native tree.
10: Grove	rimu	New Zealand / Aotearoa native tree.
10: Grove	rewarewa	New Zealand / Aotearoa native tree.
10: Grove	karaka	New Zealand / Aotearoa native tree.
10: Grove	tarata	New Zealand / Aotearoa native tree.
10: Grove	detritus	The organic debris formed from the decay of organisms; disintegrated or eroded matter.
10: Grove	*The Desolation Of Smaug*	A 2013 film directed by Peter Jackson based on J.R.R. Tolkien's *The Hobbit*. Smaug was a dragon.
10: Grove	pīwakawaka	(Māori) New Zealand / Aotearoa native bird - a small fan tail (English name: fantail!)
10: Grove	waka	Māori watercraft, usually canoes ranging in size from small, unornamented canoes (waka tīwai) used for fishing and river travel to large, decorated war canoes (waka taua) up to 40 metres (130 ft) long.

Chapter	Word	Meaning
11: Fog	topography	Topography is the study of the forms and features of surfaces.
11: Fog	catenary or parabolic	Two curves that are similar but not identical. While a parabolic arch may resemble a catenary arch, a parabola is a quadratic function while a catenary is the hyperbolic cosine, cosh(x), a sum of two exponential functions.
12: Lost	tūī	New Zealand / Aotearoa native bird. It has two voice-boxes and makes an amazing range of sounds.
12: Lost	antiphonal	Sung or played by two groups in turn.
12: Lost	kererū	New Zealand / Aotearoa native bird, a wood pigeon.
12: Lost	Indian tala	A rhythm cycle with a specific number of beats that recur in the same pattern throughout a musical performance.
12: Lost	amorphous	Without a clearly defined shape or form.
12: Lost	mantra	A repeated word or phrase, especially in advocacy or for motivation.
13: Reminiscences	'Non sequitur'	non sequitur' refers to a conclusion that isn't aligned with previous statements.

Chapter	Word	Meaning
13: Reminiscences	pōhutukawa	New Zealand / Aotearoa native trees - the NZ Christmas tree because it has crimson flowers just before Christmas.
14: Bubbles	klicks	Kilometres
14: Bubbles	robo	Robot
14: Bubbles	frizzed	Destroyed
14: Bubbles	Zefrod	Fanciful terms: an alien planet.
14: Bubbles	Pheloh 1	Fanciful terms: an alien planet.
14: Bubbles	flox	Fanciful alien terms. A flox is an animal like a cross between a giant horse and a rhinoceros, with tusks. It runs very quickly and in Pheloh 1 they are used for sport racing (and betting on the outcome).
14: Bubbles	cryogenic	Cryogenics is the production and behaviour of materials at very low temperatures.
14: Bubbles	servo	Servo systems achieve an extremely accurate position, velocity, or torque control.
14: Bubbles	Alkywanna	Fanciful terms: the name of an alien life-form.
14: Bubbles	Meduaual	Fanciful terms: an alien planet.

Chapter	Word	Meaning
15: Pane-gyric	Panegyric	A lofty oration (or eulogy) in praise of a person.
15: Pane-gyric	hyperbaric therapies	Hyperbaric oxygen therapy (HBOT) involves breathing almost pure oxygen in a special room or small chamber.

James Stephens

James is a New Zealander. He was a
teacher, musician and music director, a
journalist and event manager – as well as a
husband, father and grandfather.
He was a voracious reader, a fluent writer
and confident speaker.

In 2015, he suffered a hemiparesis, a middle
cerebral artery territory infarct.
In a word, a stroke.

He collapsed, paralysed on his right side,
and couldn't speak or write. The hospital
intervention was rapid and his limbs were
free but his speech was absent.

He had/has aphasia.

Aphasia is the loss of a previously held ability to articulate ideas or comprehend spoken or written language, resulting from damage to the brain caused by injury or disease – in this case, a stroke.

With expert therapists in speech, music and eurhythmy he has re-invented himself. He has a positive and optimistic outlook, electing to view his stroke as a 'stroke of luck'.

"My aphasia forced me to look at my life differently. My expected biography has changed. Now, I am an author – apparently."

Printed in Great Britain
by Amazon

59167130R00142